Other Works
CRAFTING A WRITER'S LIFE: Building a Foundation

Coming Soon

The Blades of Janus
PERIHELION

Cygnian 7
NUAR
KRAL
LAR
DORN
BRON
TARN
ROM

Rate of Return

The Department of Homeworld
Security
Book Fourteen

Cassandra Chandler

Copyright Page

This book is pure fiction. All characters, places, names, and events are products of the author's imagination or used solely in a fictitious manner. Any resemblance to any people, places, things, or events that have ever existed or will ever exist is entirely coincidental.

Rate of Return
The Department of Homeworld Security, Book Fourteen
Copyright © 2020 by Cassandra Chandler
Print ISBN: 978-1-945702-62-4
Digital ISBN: 978-1-945702-61-7
Edited by Evil Eye Editing

First eBook edition: March 2021
First print edition: August 2021
10 9 8 7 6 5 4 3 2 1

cassandra-chandler.com
P.O. Box 91
Mission, Kansas 66201

Dedication

For my sister, the entrepreneur.

Don't miss out on any of the alien action.
Subscribe to Cassandra Chandler's newsletter at
cassandra-chandler.com!

Chapter One

This was not a reunion he was looking forward to.

The last time Serac had encountered—what was he calling himself now? Dean—Serac had vowed it would be the last. Yet here he was, standing in an open field near a small dwelling on a primitive planet in the middle of the night. Waiting.

His *zyln,* the elemental spirit living within him, was preoccupied with the dwelling. Something about it unsettled them both.

Serac eyed the entrance, which was situated a few feet above the ground on a wooden porch. On the second level of the building, there was a row of dark windows, one of which kept drawing his attention.

He could easily leap onto the porch's roof and pry open the window to get inside. But why did he want to?

Footsteps crunched in the snow behind him. Serac turned to see a tall, thin humanoid. At least, that was the form Dean was borrowing. Serac was one of the few people who had actually seen a Scorpiian in his natural form and lived to tell about it.

"I wasn't sure you'd come." Dean's voice was lighter in

this form. Smoother.

For the moment, Dean's light brown hair stuck up in unruly waves. He was dressed in some sort of uniform with matching dark pants and a jacket over a deep blue shirt that was unbuttoned at the throat.

If that was the garb that people in this small settlement wore, Serac would stand out. He was wearing jeans and a T-shirt, as well as a thicker jacket that was almost unbearably warm.

The air was crisp and cool around him. In other circumstances, he'd strip naked, shift his form, and run through the woods to enjoy the coolness of the ecosystem. His *zyln* rumbled approval deep within.

This place reminded him of Centaurus-10.

It reminded him of home.

"Go ahead," Dean said, nodding toward a particularly tall drift of snow. "Weather patterns in this area are highly variable. You might not have another chance to enjoy this sort of environment. Unless, of course, you've decided to join me."

Serac wasn't ready to confront or commit, so he said, "That's an interesting form you're borrowing. It almost looks Sadirian."

Dean shrugged one shoulder. "It doesn't really make a difference what you want to call this form. Earthlings and Sadirians are genetically almost identical, unlike you Centaurans, who only *look* Sadirian. Well, sometimes."

Serac felt his hackles rise, the hair on the back of his neck standing on end. Dean was baiting him. But Serac wasn't the impulsive thug he used to be.

"You said you'd found a prize," Serac said.

"I have."

"Convince me of its worth. You have three minutes."

Dean smirked and even chuckled. "So in charge. And here I'd heard that you were bowing to a *Lyrian* lately." Dean's lip curled as he said the word. "When you and I worked together, you bowed to no one."

Except my conscience—and even that took too long.

"Two minutes left," Serac said.

"Fine. I've encountered a life form on this planet that seems completely harmless. They're small, furred, with four legs—like most Earth wildlife. The humans call them cats. The Earthlings think they've domesticated them."

"You don't agree."

"No," Dean said. "At best, the cats allow humans to cohabitate with them. They're extraordinary creatures. I was attacked by half a dozen of them recently. They were harboring a toxin in their claws and bite that required almost an hour in a purification chamber for my body to purge."

For Dean to have needed so much time in the healing chamber, the toxin had to have been particularly problematic for his physiology.

"So, what?" Serac said. "You've called me here to

intimidate them for you? Maybe rough them up a little?"

"I plan to capture some," Dean said.

"And you need me for that."

"Need? No." A muscle in Dean's jaw flexed and his smirk disappeared. "I'm providing you with an opportunity. Don't be so stupid that you can't see it."

A growl built low in Serac's throat. He forced it down.

"These creatures are valuable enough that a Sadirian was trying to harvest a DNA sample from them for the Coalition's scientists," Dean said.

Serac snorted. "Sadirians will take DNA from anything. They're obsessive about collecting it."

"True, but this Sadirian was working with a Vegan."

That prompted a quick intake of breath that Serac couldn't quite hide. Dean's smirk returned.

"I thought that might catch your attention," Dean said.

Serac had heard rumors that the Vegans had made an appearance during the Battle of Sadr-4. He'd dismissed it as propaganda from the Coalition of Planets in its effort to maintain their control over most of the sentients in the galaxy.

It had to be a lie meant to scare everyone into staying within their rule. Their High Council had been obliterated and their entire home system destroyed.

Serac clenched his fists as he thought of his people's role in that. The air around him grew colder.

"Vegans are a myth," he said.

"Believe what you will. But know that the DNA of these Earth cats is a high prize—as are the creatures themselves."

"If you want their DNA, why not get it yourself?" Serac asked. "You must have had some available, given that they bit you."

"The samples were tainted by my body's immune response." Dean went on, his voice rising with excitement. "These creatures are unlike anything you've ever encountered. Some of them seem docile while others are outright murderous. And they can switch from one state to the next without giving any sign to their change in temperament."

"Sounds like you have much in common," Serac said.

Dean snorted. "I'm willing to let our past remain in the past. Together, we can capture these animals and market them as vicious guardian beasts. Imagine if we, too, could win their favor and then provide them as pets throughout the galaxy? One moment, the beast is calmly resting upon its beloved owner's lap. The next, it's sprung to attack. We can modify its natural microbiome to make its bite and scratch even more dangerous."

"These all sound like stories for the hearth fires," Serac said.

Dean scowled. "I am not plying you with children's tales. Vegans are real. Cats are real."

"Then capture one and sell it. You don't need me."

"If it were that simple, I wouldn't have called you in the first place. We need someone who understands them. Someone who can control them and teach us how to induce their docile state. And I've found the perfect Earthling to help us. She just needs some convincing."

Dean was talking about abducting a sentient. And from what Serac knew of the Scorpiian, he would absolutely go through with his plan.

The hairs on Serac's nape rose again. His *zyln* grew more alert within, the sense of impending danger growing.

"The human who lives in this dwelling runs a place called a 'pet parlor.' Her name is Kimmy and she is a specialist in controlling animals—including cats."

Cygnus-X, he's planning to do this now.

"If we can acquire her, she will enable us to capture the cats and train them," Dean said. "We just need to persuade her to assist us."

Serac knew what Dean had in mind when he spoke of "persuading" sentients. Serac wouldn't be part of it. And he couldn't let this happen.

"Your plan has one obstacle," he said.

"And what is that?"

Serac's *zyln* rose up in him, energy coursing through his body as it began the change.

"Me."

Chapter Two

A piercing howl woke Kimmy from her sound sleep. At first, she thought it was a continuation of her amazing dream—a lovely side-effect of reading the latest paranormal shifter romance in her favorite series right before bed.

But then she heard the unmistakable growls and barks of dogs fighting. *Real* dogs. And something sounded off about one of them.

She threw off the pile of comforters and quilts she'd buried herself beneath and flung herself out of bed. The floor was freezing, and for the millionth time she wished she could stand sleeping in socks—or really anything more than a long nightshirt and undies.

"Cold, cold, cold," she chanted, hopping on one foot, then the other as she scrambled for her oversized, fur-lined house-boots.

She grabbed her glasses and pushed them onto her face. After fumbling for the lights in the hallway, she ran downstairs, then grabbed a coat in the kitchen and pulled it on.

As she headed out the back door, she picked up her

broom, just in case. She had a way with animals, but these dogs sounded…

Enormous. Oh my God, they're huge.

And they weren't dogs. Not like any she'd seen before.

She froze on her back porch, trying to make sense of what she was seeing, wondering if she was still dreaming.

At first, she thought they might be wolves. But wolves weren't so big.

They also didn't glow.

Or have tentacles.

The larger animal had five enormous eyes on its face, making it look like a cross between a wolf and a bug. The tentacles rippling along its back added to the…not-wolfness of it. That and the purple and green fur covering its body.

It was fighting what looked a lot like a gigantic wolf. His pelt was pure white and glowed with a silvery light that trailed along behind him as he moved.

If it wasn't for the fact that they were obviously trying to kill each other—and that one of them looked like a nightmare—the sight would have been…magical.

"Fairies," she whispered.

The glowing wolf looked over at her. His opponent took advantage of the momentary distraction.

Kimmy screamed as the nightmare-wolf latched onto the glowing wolf's neck and shook, hard. Without thinking, she ran forward, waving her broom and yelling.

In some part of her brain, she realized how foolish it was—how dangerous and futile—but she couldn't stop herself. She wouldn't.

She charged at them full speed. The moment she reached the pair, she started whacking the nightmare-wolf as hard as she could, over and over again. It released the glowing wolf and snapped at her, its teeth clacking loudly inches away from her face.

She screamed again, but didn't back off. With all her strength, she hit it soundly on the head with her broom.

"Bad dog!" she yelled.

What the hell am I doing?

The nightmare-wolf staggered back and shook itself. It growled, staring at her with calculating intelligence in its eyes.

"Back off!" Kimmy said.

She pushed as much authority as she could into her order, jabbing the broom in its direction. To her complete shock, the nightmare-wolf actually backed up a step. It looked between her and the glowing wolf, then turned and loped away.

"Oh my God, I can't believe that worked."

The glowing wolf started letting out hacking coughs, his legs shaking, then he fell onto his side.

"No, no, no." Kimmy dropped her broom and knelt in the snow next to him, burying her fingers in his fur.

She couldn't feel any injuries, but he was already so

cold. The poor thing.

"Hang on," she said. "I'll help you."

She shed her giant coat and spread it out on the ground behind the wolf. The cold hit her immediately, making her teeth chatter.

"Oh my God," she said. "What am I doing now?"

She shook her head, answering herself. "I'm helping an animal in need. That's what I'm doing. And talking to myself as I do it. As usual."

The wolf tried to get up, which gave her a chance to scoot the fabric underneath him. When he fell back over, he landed right in the middle of her coat.

As big as her coat was, the wolf was bigger. Still, with the slick snow beneath him, she was able to drag him to her house.

She had piled a bunch of snow up next to her porch when she'd shoveled the walkways earlier in the day. Hopefully, there was enough packed in to hold their weight.

She sucked in a breath and ran toward the slope, tugging the wolf after her. The makeshift ramp worked like a charm. On the porch, she didn't stop, but kept up their momentum until she had him through the kitchen door.

"I'm so glad I left that open," she said.

Snow and ice scattered across the tile, but she didn't care. At least it was warmer inside. She could mop up the mess later.

Rising to close the door, she noticed another glowing creature. This one was bright red, his glow so intense, it almost hurt to look at him. Whatever this was, he was tiny.

And fast.

She tried to slam the door, but before it shut, the furry little thing bolted into her kitchen, climbing up the drawers and onto the counter. He knocked over several containers as he made his way to her cabinets. When he reached the top, she could hear him running back and forth, chittering angrily, the red glow of his fur streaking along the ceiling.

"What now?" she asked.

She had left her broom outside, but the little guy had knocked a spatula onto the counter. Kimmy picked it up and kept it ready, just in case he tried to jump at her.

"Settle down," she said. "I have enough to deal with already."

The wolf seemed really out of it, but made a chuffing noise. She dropped back to her knees next to him. Her hand went to his head automatically, years of practice and instinct taking over. She gently petted him, trying to keep at least one of her strange visitors happy.

"It's okay," she murmured. "It's okay."

His coat was still so cold, even with the door shut. She tried to pull more of her coat around him, but he was just too big. His eyes had rolled shut, but his breath was coming more easily.

"That's it," she cooed, stroking his fur. "Just breathe. You're going to be okay."

Movement from the top of the cabinets was her only warning that the little guy had decided to join them. He spread his limbs—all *six* of them—stretching the skin that connected them and glided down to land on the wolf's side.

The tiny creature was only letting out little squeaks now, so she kept up with the soothing talk. He also started changing color, oscillating between red and yellow.

"It really is okay," she said. "I'm only trying to help."

The color-changing critter settled into a pale pink color, paws burrowing into the wolf's pelt. He poked his head up, staring at her with huge, black-and-pink eyes.

"You are just adorable," she said. "Which I hope isn't an insult."

She dared to reach out and gently run her fingertip over his head. He blinked a few times, making a quizzical noise, then closed his eyes and started to sort of purr.

"Is this your friend?" She gave the wolf another gentle pat. "I'm going to help, okay?"

Her tiny guest looked like a sugar glider, only with two feathery antennae coming off the top of his head. His fur was even softer than the wolf's.

This has *to be a fairy. And that means…*

She looked back to the wolf, gingerly feeling around his neck. He let out another chuff, which was way better than the hacking noises he had made earlier. She thought back to how the other wolf-thing had looked at her with uncanny intelligence in its eyes.

Excitement shot through her. Could it be?

"Please be a werewolf," she murmured.

A hot guy werewolf.

She managed not to say that thought out loud.

The fairy glider made an indignant squeak, then scurried up Kimmy's arm and nestled at the base of her neck. She could feel several of his arms holding onto her hair to stay in place.

The wolf's fur glowed more brightly, then pulled back into his skin. His muscles popped and joints cracked as they shifted into a humanoid shape—an absolutely masculine humanoid shape.

Kimmy sat back on her heels to give him space, but stayed close in case he needed help. Not at all because hot werewolf shifter romances were her absolute favorite genre of books and she prayed that she was living one at that very moment.

The man raised himself up on his hands and knees, breathing heavily. The muscles of his back flexed with the movement. He was beefier than she usually liked, but watching the light glint off of his richly tanned skin, she didn't have any complaints.

Give the guy a break, Kimmy. He just got his ass kicked.

Although, he'd been doing okay until she'd distracted him. Hopefully, he wouldn't hold that against her.

Hopefully, he'd hold other things against her.

Chiding herself yet again, she reached out and gently touched his shoulder.

"Are you okay?" she asked.

He jerked away, landing hard on his backside and staring at her with wide eyes—amber eyes that went perfectly with his short, raven-black hair. As he moved, he grabbed her coat, draping it over his lap to cover himself.

His lips were full, his eyebrows dark slashes above his eyes. He had a strong jawline, too, matching his physique. There was a haunted quality to his eyes that drew her in.

"It's okay." She held out her hands in a calming gesture.

She realized she was still holding the spatula. They both stared at it. Could he think it was a weapon? She tossed it away, just in case.

"I'm not going to hurt you," she said.

He swallowed hard. She could see his throat work. Then he licked those lush lips.

Her heart beat hard against her ribs and her mind reeled, wondering what his first words to her would be. She leaned forward as he opened his mouth to speak.

"Are you insane?" he said.

Chapter Three

The Earthling's dark eyebrows rose above the thick-framed lenses she wore. The frames sat on her face a bit crooked.

Her lips parted and closed repeatedly. Serac tried not to focus on them. It was more challenging than it should have been. They looked soft and warm.

Everything about her looked soft and warm—from her large, forest-green eyes, to the immense boots she wore.

He knew her hands were soft and warm. Waking up to her gentle touch had been…pleasant. His *zyln* urged him to reach for her hands and hold them.

He refused.

"Excuse me?" she said.

"Why?"

She blinked a few times. "What?"

"What are you asking me to excuse?"

"I'm not…" She let out an exasperated sound, then straightened the frame of her lenses. "I'm not insane!"

"You intervened in my battle. With a stick."

"It was a *broom*. And if I'd known I was running into a fight between a fairy and a shifter, I would have brought silver or iron or something."

He felt like the gravity in the room had suddenly reversed, his stomach lurching. Even his *zyln* stilled within.

She knew what he was? Or, perhaps she was referring to Dean as the shifter and thought that Serac was... whatever a fairy was. Either way, why in the name of the Frozen Clans wasn't she terrified?

"Because she is brave," his *zyln* thought.

No one could be that brave. Could they?

"Why does she think silver would be better than a stick?"

His *zyln* paused for a moment before thinking, *"Brave and...confused."*

This Earthling filled Serac's mind with questions. It was unsettling.

"You're not afraid of me?" Serac said.

Her expression softened. "No, I'm not afraid."

"And you know what I am?" His heart pounded and his mouth went dry. Strangely, how she answered was important to him. He tried to shake off the feeling, but his *zyln* was sitting up within him, intently focused on her response.

"I do," she said. "You're a werewolf."

"A what wolf?" his *zyln* thought.

"A what wolf?" he asked their question out loud.

He knew the latter part of the word—which made

sense, given his *zyln's* form. Serac had been warned about the Earth lifeforms that his other form resembled before setting off on his mission. But he didn't understand the "where" part. Did it have something to do with translocation?

"A werewolf," she repeated.

"I'm not familiar with that word." It seemed impossible that Earthlings could know what the Centaurans were— what they could do.

"You're a person who can turn into a wolf."

And there was the impossible, staring at him from a beautiful face through thick lenses.

"You aren't supposed to know about me," he said.

She smiled, ducking her head, then started to laugh. His cheeks tugged, his mouth twitching as if it wanted to smile back. He couldn't remember the last time he'd felt such a thing. His breath stilled within his chest.

"Stop it," she said, looking off to the side and lifting her shoulders up to her ears. "That tickles."

His mirth fled. What was she talking about?

She reached up under her hair and pulled out Payback, the parcel Serac's captain, Hank, had instructed him to deliver to Earth as part of his assignment. It was meant as a gift for Hank's newest sibling. Serac had instructed the parcel to remain on his ship.

"How did you get here?" Serac snapped.

Payback stuck his tongue out at Serac, then rolled over

so that the Earthling had better access to his stomach. Whatever she was doing, the parcel seemed to be enjoying it immensely. He shifted through mellow blues and happy pinks before settling into his natural magenta shade, glowing softly.

"He's beautiful," the Earthling said. "What's his name?" Her eyes widened and she shook her head. "Oh, no. I'm sorry. I didn't mean to ask."

"For his name?" Did names have more significance on Earth than Serac realized?

"You may have his name," Serac said. "It's Payback."

"You don't owe me anything. I was happy to help."

Again, he had no idea what she was talking about. She was utterly baffling.

And utterly fascinating.

To be as clear as possible, he said, "The parcel's name is Payback."

The Earthling looked around them, then leaned closer. "What parcel?"

Serac sucked in a breath, desiring to yell or howl or... something. He wanted to throw open the door, shift into his other form, and go for a long run in the deep snow that covered the surrounding lands. Perhaps that would clear his head.

And yet, the idea of leaving this Earthling behind unsettled him.

"We must stay with her," his *zyln* thought. *"We must*

protect her."

The air around them shimmered and her breath came out as puffs of fog. She shivered, pulling Payback closer to her chest as if to warm him.

At least she didn't know that much. Parcels were from the icy Lyrian homeworld—one of the few inhabited planets even colder than Centaurus-10.

Perhaps that was why Serac was so unnerved by her presence. She seemed to know so much more about him than she should.

Slowly releasing his breath, he calmed himself again. The air warmed around them.

"The creature in your lap is called a parcel," Serac said. "His name is Payback."

"Oh," she said. Her eyes widened again and she nodded. "Ohhhhh."

The parcel let out a cooing trill, then closed his eyes. His antennae drooped, and a soft hum sounded with each breath.

He was asleep.

That was not good.

"He has chosen her," his *zyln* thought.

"What's wrong?" The Earthling was watching Serac's face with keen interest. Part of him warmed at the thought. Another questioned her motives.

"Parcels do not trust lightly," he said.

"Well, maybe this one just has good taste." She smiled

at him, and he felt it like a thump to his chest.

"He trusts you," Serac said.

"Okay."

"I have chosen her, too."

"It is not okay," Serac said, both to her and his *zyln*. He forced himself to focus on the parcel, and not the impossible idea that his *zyln* wanted him to bond with this Earthling. "Payback was recently removed from his companion. I was to present him to his new master so they could imprint."

"Master?" she said. She lifted Payback closer to her face and pressed a kiss to his forehead. "I don't like the sound of that. *Friend* sounds much better to me."

Words stuck in Serac's throat. Bravery, beauty, and kindness… His *zyln* paced within him. He had to stifle a growl that rose up in his chest—resist the urge to reach for her and draw her into his lap.

"She is ours," his *zyln* thought.

"She can't be."

Serac pushed the thought away. "Whatever you wish to call him, he has imprinted with you."

"What?" Distress flashed across her features. "But… I don't want you to get in trouble. I'm sorry, I—"

"Never apologize for showing something kindness," Serac said. "But parcels are incredibly loyal and protective of the sentients they imprint with. You're stuck with this one for the foreseeable future."

"How am I going to explain what he is? I mean, *I'm* not even sure what he is." She lifted the parcel to her cheek and snuggled against him, then kissed his head as he let out a contented coo.

Serac couldn't believe how well she was adapting to this circumstance. Most sentients would be terrified of everything they'd just seen—even if they were aware of the existence of other interstellar life forms.

Earthlings were not supposed to know about them.

"I'll make sure my captain understands," he said.

"Captain…"

Her brow furrowed again. She looked down at Payback and ran a fingertip over his antennae. The parcel twitched in his sleep, yawned, and rolled over, draping three of his limbs over her arm.

The Earthling let out a gentle snort, nodding as if she was coming to some sort of internal understanding—one that she didn't like. Her gaze was low and guarded. He wished to see her eyes, to try to read what she was feeling.

How could it matter to him so much already?

Her shoulders slumped. "You're aliens."

Didn't she already know that? Why him being an alien should disappoint her was yet another mystery. The more time he spent in this Earthling's presence, the more questions he had.

And the more he longed for answers.

Payback rolled over again. She looked down at the

parcel lying in her lap and started wiggling her fingertips through the fur on his belly.

"Who's so cute, though?" she said, her voice more subdued.

Payback half-woke, chittering happily. He grabbed her finger with most of his limbs and started doing the same movement against her skin. She giggled, her smile returning.

"You like tickles?" she asked. "You're so good at it. But I'm a master, too." Then she kept repeating, "tickles," while wriggling her fingers against him.

"Parcels are adept at locating nerve clusters in life forms," Serac said, uncertain why he was sharing the information with her.

"Are you?" she asked the parcel.

His hackles rose. How could he be jealous of a parcel?

"Are you good at tickles?" she repeated.

The parcel made a chittering sound that melded with her own laughter.

Prickles of warmth rose from the base of Serac's spine, spreading out across his back in a wave that caused his hairs to stand on end. The sensation was...pleasant.

"What's your name?" He had to be certain she was Dean's target, though seeing how she had won over Payback, Serac didn't doubt that this was the animal trainer Dean sought.

"I suppose it's okay to tell you since you're not a fairy,"

she murmured. "My name is Kimmy. What's yours?"

"Serac."

"Yeah, that sounds about right."

He wondered what she would have considered a wrong answer. "What's a fairy?"

She focused intently on the parcel, delaying for so long he wasn't sure she would answer him. "Fairies are magical beings that exist in the stories we tell here. On Earth."

"But you think they're real."

"Not really."

"Then why did you think we were fairies?"

"Hello. Shapeshifting hottie with a glowing pink parcel." Her cheeks reddened. "That didn't sound right. Anyway, werewolves are a kind of Fae being. It was kind of hard to explain to myself what I was seeing otherwise. Until, you know. *Aliens*."

"But you knew about aliens before our arrival," he said.

He knew that some humans had been brought in to their "Department of Homeworld Security," but it seemed unlikely that his first encounter with an Earthling would be with a member. Then again, perhaps that was part of why she'd been Dean's target.

"My best friend's grandpa has been trading with a pair of Lyrians for decades," Kimmy said.

Serac was stunned. Was she talking about Hank's parents, Craig and Barbara? And, if so, did that mean she was connected with one of their sources?

This could be an even better opportunity than he'd thought.

His *zyln* rumbled within him, sending waves of disapproval through Serac.

"We have a mission."

A surge of protectiveness displaced all other emotions. Apparently, his *zyln* had a mission of its own—one that centered around this human.

Kimmy started speaking again, drawing all of his attention.

"Harbor—that's the name of the town you're in, in case you didn't know," she said. "Anyway, Harbor is under consideration by the Department of Homeworld Security —because apparently we have one of those now—for becoming the first place on Earth where aliens can come and visit us. It's a really big deal, but it's all very secret and not many people in the town know yet. We're supposed to have some vote about it when they're ready to approach everyone."

How could she say so much with so few pauses? Serac had never met such a talkative sentient. And yet, he found himself intently focused on every word.

"Plus, there was this whole thing with a Scorpiian," she said. "Not the bug, but the shapeshifting..."

Her eyebrows lifted again and her eyes widened as she stared at him.

"I'm not a Scorpiian," he rushed to reassure her.

Though, with all she knew, if she found out what Serac really was, perhaps she'd *wish* he was a Scorpiian.

"The creature you attacked earlier is a Scorpiian," he said. "He had assumed the form of a quryl."

A clever move, since the quryl was indigenous to Centaurus-10. If Serac hadn't been hoping that Dean would give up and run off to regroup, Serac still could have probably frozen Dean in place. But while in that form, Dean was semi-immune to the cold himself.

"Wait a minute," Kimmy said. "Was that the same guy who was after the cats we were boarding for Mrs. Simpkins at the pet parlor?"

"He is on Earth looking to obtain cats." Serac thought it best not to go too deeply into the details. "I don't know which ones specifically."

"Hmph." Kimmy shook her head, then looked up at him and smiled. Her cheeks turned pink again. "Were you sent here to protect me or something?"

That hadn't been within his original mission parameters, but now that he was here, he couldn't deny it had become part of his personal objectives. Watching the flush creep down her throat and disappear beneath the neckline of her garment, he tried not to think of just how *personal* those objectives were becoming.

He looked away and cleared his throat. "That is my intention."

"Oh," she said. "Neat."

He could protect her and still fulfill his other objectives. If he could establish a connection with Craig and Barbara's source, this would become one of his most successful scouting missions.

"I believe it would assist my mission objectives to meet this grandpa," he said. "Could you introduce me?"

"Sure." She looked out the window at the dark sky. "But after it's light out, okay? Even with a werewolf helping me out—sorry, *space*-werewolf—I'd rather not be running around in the dark with that Scorpiian out there."

"Agreed," he said.

Chapter Four

Kimmy stifled a yawn as she poured cereal into three bowls at her round kitchen table. She still couldn't believe that a werewolf had slept on her couch last night—after she'd found him some of her brother's clothes to wear. The parcel clinging to her shoulder was a helpful reminder that she wasn't dreaming.

And even though they were aliens and not the Fae beings she'd always dreamed of meeting, she knew that this was the beginning of the greatest adventure of her life.

Something about Serac drew her in. It wasn't just his looks or physique, though that alone would be enough to have her drooling.

He had this energy about him that almost felt like… Well, like gravity. She wasn't quite sure why—beyond the obvious—but she wanted to be closer to him.

She had to admit, there was also some kind of crazy chemistry going on. At least, from her side of things. When he came close, her body lit up like a lightning storm.

She'd barely managed to sleep the night before—lying awake and wondering about too many things. Where was

Serac from? What was his planet like? Was someone back there waiting for him?

Down, girl.

She scoffed at herself as she sealed up the box and put the cereal back on top of the fridge. While her arm was outstretched, Payback ran up along it and disappeared behind the boxes.

"Try not to get in trouble," she said.

"Trouble?"

She turned as Serac entered from the back door, a jacket and tattered clothing in his hands. He also had her broom, which he propped up in the corner near the door.

Kimmy stammered for a full thirty seconds before managing, "Parcel. I was talking to Payback."

"I see." Serac walked to the table and draped the clothing over the back of one of the chairs. "Parcels are notorious for getting into things they shouldn't."

"Or out of them," Kimmy said.

Serac stared at her blankly.

"You said Payback was supposed to stay in your ship," she explained.

The corner of Serac's mouth twitched a little. She was so close to getting him to smile.

"One of the reasons they're given to nestlings is to keep the new spawn's appendages busy," he said.

"Lyrians do have a lot of limbs. I guess I'll just have to keep Payback busy with tickles." She wiggled her fingers in the air.

Serac's perpetual scowl deepened and his brow furrowed. What would it take to make him smile?

She got out the milk and headed for the table. "So, where are you from?"

Under normal circumstances, that would seem like the lamest question in the world. These were far from normal circumstances.

She poured the milk on their cereal—a generic brand of the kind that made the crackling sound when it first became wet.

"I..." Amazingly, his eyebrows knitted even closer together as he stared at the cereal. "I'd rather not say."

"Really? Why not?"

Her question wrested his attention from the cereal for a moment.

"I'd rather not say," he said.

"Oh, okay."

Kimmy, master of probing, overly personal questions.

She struggled to find something to fill the awkward silence, aside from the noise of the cereal. As it turned out, she didn't need to.

He pointed at the bowl closest to him. "What is that?"

"It's cereal," she said, heading back to the fridge to put the milk away. "We can't go to Marvin's on an empty stomach. Although, now that I think of it, he always feeds Sabrina and me when we visit him. Sabrina is his granddaughter and my best friend. We run the 'Look Again Pet Parlor' together."

Her mouth kept going, and she couldn't seem to stop herself. As usual.

"I know it's a weird name, but one of our specialties is working with animals that aren't the best-behaved," she said. "A lot of the time, people just need to look at their pets with fresh eyes. Well, and maybe a little professional insight. Plus, there's the whole, 'We make your pets so pretty, people will look again,' thing. Like, do a double-take. And as an added bonus, it subliminally suggests to people that they 'look again' at our pet parlor, in case they were about to make the mistake of choosing another."

Why was she giving him the sales pitch? Did she think he'd come to Earth to get his parcel groomed?

His eyebrows hiked up his forehead. At least the furrow was gone.

She had just kind of unloaded on him—a trait that had cost her many a boyfriend in the past. And regular friend, really.

"This is food?" he asked, as if the whole tangent about the parlor hadn't happened.

Maybe she hadn't chased him off with her chattiness. Yet.

"Yeah." She laughed. "It's good. Try it."

He cocked his head at an angle and backed away from the table. Kimmy burst out laughing, and the furrow came right back again.

"I'm sorry," she said. "Just seeing a big, strong guy like you intimidated by a bowl of cereal is kind of funny."

"I'm not intimidated," he said. "I'm wary."

She feigned a serious expression. "Oh, right. Very good, then."

She sat and picked up her spoon. After shoveling a good-sized bite into her mouth, she made some yummy sounds to show him it was okay.

"It's delicious," she said, once she managed to swallow. "You should try some."

"No, thanks."

She shrugged. "More for me and Payback. Do you think it's safe for him to eat?"

"All beings from Lyra have incredibly resilient constitutions."

"I'll take that as a yes." She turned toward the fridge and said, "Payback. Here, boy."

The parcel appeared between two boxes, his antennae pointing straight up as he chirruped. Waves of pretty pale blue rippled through his fur.

"Breakfast," Kimmy said, pointing at his bowl.

The parcel leapt from the fridge, opening all six legs to glide to the table. The moment he touched down, he hopped into the bowl.

"Oh, shoot," she said, grabbing a napkin.

Payback's head popped up through the cereal. His

cheeks were stuffed full as he chewed, and milk dribbled from his nose.

"Payback," she mock-scolded. "Your table manners are awful."

She glanced over at Serac and smiled. He was still scowling at her, as if he didn't know what to make of her. Not many people did. But dangit, she really wanted to see him smile.

She reached for Payback to clean him up, but he ducked beneath the cereal before she could grab him. She should have used the smaller bowls.

"Payback, you rapscallion," she said. "Get out of there."

His head surfaced again, glowing sky blue. Using four of his paws, he started shoving cereal into his mouth and chewing incredibly fast.

"Slow down," she said. "You're going to choke."

"Parcels are sturdier than that." Serac was still far from the table, and it was starting to annoy Kimmy.

"Would you please at least sit down?" she said. "We're supposed to be having breakfast together."

He eyed the cereal as if it might bite him, then the chair with equal dread. After a few moments, he sat.

"There, was that so hard?" She picked up his spoon and handed it to him.

Their fingers brushed, and even that slight contact was enough to send a rush of goosebumps along her arms. He had to feel something, too. He sat up straighter, his chest puffing up as he held his breath.

The same thing had happened a few times the night before. Just being close to him sent her body into overdrive.

She'd never experienced anything similar. It was like something out of one of her books.

Which meant she was probably imagining it— perceiving what she wanted to perceive.

"Eat something," she said. "Oh, and you should know I'm a master at nagging people."

"I don't know what *nagging* means."

Lucky me.

"You'll figure it out," she said. "Now eat."

He took a cautious bite, eating as slowly as Payback was hurrying. His brow knit, yet again, and then smoothed.

"This is good," he said.

Smiling at achieving at least that victory, she said, "I know."

Serac finished his breakfast methodically, while she and Payback snarfed theirs. He watched her with an intensity that made her wonder if perhaps she wasn't imagining things after all.

When they finished eating, she said, "We can head to Marvin's now. If you're ready."

Serac nodded. "If I may ask a boon, please don't

mention that I can change my shape."

"I wasn't planning on it, but sure. I know I talk a lot, but I really can control myself about important topics. Like the whole 'aliens are real' thing. I've known for weeks and haven't told a soul. I don't want to mess this up for anyone."

He nodded, his shoulders relaxing a bit.

"Is it a problem that you can shapeshift?" she asked. "I mean, I can tell Marvin you're not a Scorpiian."

"Scorpiians have used their abilities to become bounty hunters and assassins. They are very good at what they do. Unfortunately, their success has engendered distrust for all sentients capable of changing their shape."

"That's ridiculous," Kimmy said. "Just because one group misuses their abilities doesn't mean everyone with similar gifts will."

His mouth opened as if he was about to speak, but then he snapped it shut and looked away.

"What?" she asked.

He shook his head, but kept casting glances at her from the corner of his eye.

"Wary," he had said. She had a feeling he wasn't just talking about the cereal. It seemed to be part of his makeup. Hearing him talk about how shifters were seen, she could see why.

"I like to wear black," Kimmy said.

He looked her up and down, as if confirming her

statement by reviewing her completely black ensemble. Black long-sleeved shirt. Black pants. Black boots. Black glasses. Black hair, though that was natural.

"Everyone takes one look at me, and they think they know who I am," Kimmy said. "There's a stereotype around here that people who wear black are moody or antisocial. A lot of people have given me grief over it or been put off by it, I guess. But I just like to wear black. What I'm using too many words to say—again—is that people need to let go of their preconceptions."

"I'm not even from this world. How could I have preconceptions?"

She smiled at him and even laughed. "That's part of what makes you so great."

Oh, that was an over-share. But the way his features softened, his lips parting and that furrow retreating again, it was worth the momentary embarrassment. Besides, she meant it.

"My best friend basically looks like a doll," Kimmy said. "Everyone thinks that she must be so sweet when they first see her, but she's likely to rip off your head if you cross her."

He recoiled, one hand going to his right hip. Maybe he usually kept a ray gun there. Kimmy laughed again and reached out to touch his arm.

Any excuse…

"With her words," she said, emphatically. "Not for

real."

Slowly, he moved his hand back to the table. She gripped it and gave it a squeeze. When she tried to let go, he held on, and even interlaced their fingers.

Her skin rose in goosebumps again and her heartbeat picked up. She wondered if he could hear it and added that to the list of millions of questions she had for him. Her cheeks prickled with heat that spread down her throat and chest and...other places.

She had to clear her throat before saying, "I just want you to know that I don't have any preconceptions, either. You start off with a clean slate with me. Just the werewolf guy I found trying to chase off a Scorpiian in my backyard. Sorry, space-werewolf."

The corner of Serac's mouth quirked. She was so close to getting him to smile. But then Payback jumped out of his bowl and shook his fur, milk and cereal going everywhere.

"Payback!" Kimmy yelled.

She pulled her hand free of Serac's grip, which she noticed he seemed a bit hesitant to allow. Then she grabbed Payback and headed for the sink.

"We're going to have to teach you some manners, aren't we?" She glanced over at Serac.

He stared at her intently again—or rather, *still*. She really liked it.

He cleared his throat and nodded. "Yes, I suppose we

are."

Chapter Five

Watching Kimmy clean up the parcel caused warmth to flood through Serac's system yet again. It seemed to be happening more often as he interacted with her.

She had shared her den with him, clothed him, and now she shared her food.

His *zyln* continued to pace within him, as it had from the moment he'd awakened to her touch. Each physical contact increased his desire for *more* contact. More intimacy, on every level.

He reminded himself yet again that she couldn't understand the significance of her gestures. On Centaurus-10, everything she was doing was a prelude to forming a mate bond.

She couldn't possibly be interested in bonding with him. That knowledge did nothing to stop his urges to touch her, to kiss her, to claim her.

He took a deep breath and let it out slowly. He would control his instincts, no matter how his *zyln* howled within him.

The challenge was that he actually…liked her. It had been so long since he liked an individual, he was having trouble adapting to it.

She was brave and playful and caring. For a moment, he wondered if she *might* consider sharing her life with a shifter.

He shook himself internally. She might seem more accepting than most, but once she learned more about his people and his own past... There were some things no one could see past. He should stop torturing himself with "what-ifs."

"We should go." He stood abruptly, almost knocking over his chair.

Kimmy glanced at him briefly and smiled, still giving most of her attention to Payback. She had wrapped him in a towel after cleaning him and was drying him off gently.

"Just a second," she said, fluffing up the parcel's fur as he made more contented cooing sounds. "Aaand, done. I wish I had a ribbon for your antennae. They're so cute. And you're so cute."

Payback rested four of his paws on her arm, gazing up with loving adoration.

Serac could understand the sentiment. He shook the thought away. It was ridiculous to be having such thoughts —much too soon. And yet, a true mating bond would come on quickly.

In all of his past relationships, he had never experienced the faintest stirrings of wanting to form a bond. Was she feeling anything toward him as well? If she was, then it was a sure sign that they were meant to be mated.

In any case, she wasn't Centauran. Rushing things could scare her off. Or worse—bind her in a relationship she would eventually come to regret.

Centauran bonds were permanent. Their souls would be linked together for the rest of their lives.

"As it should be." He felt another flood of determination from his *zyln*. Apparently, it was absolutely fine with that idea.

Serac was still adjusting.

He picked up his jacket and put it on. Kimmy finally stood, lifting Payback to her shoulder as she did. The parcel settled into the collar of her jacket, burrowing beneath her hair.

"It's going to be fun driving with this little guy riding like this," she said.

"Parcels usually burrow into the fur of their Lyrian. He's most likely resting there because it's the closest approximation."

"That makes sense. Still, if I wasn't afraid he'd get too cold, I'd make him sit in the back."

"Lyra is an ice world, like mine," he said. "We don't feel the cold as you do."

"Oh, wow. That must be nice. I can never seem to get warm enough."

Once they were bonded, she would never feel cold

again. It would be a boon for her.

He shook away the thought. That was not where he should be focusing.

"He can stay on my shoulder anyway—I kind of like him there." She gently prodded Payback, and said, "But no sudden movements, okay? You don't want to distract the driver. You might not feel the cold, but those roads are icy and we don't want to be in an accident."

She led them out the back door and to a smaller building near her house. Inside was a land transport—a car. Once they were seated in it, she pressed a button, and a large door opened on the wall behind them, much like in a hangar bay. In a few moments, they were underway.

Serac examined the surroundings as much as he could while they traveled along the roads. Her car slipped a few times, prompting words that his translation session hadn't covered, but he assumed were expletives. He saved his questions and let her concentrate on piloting the vehicle.

The area was thick with trees and other plant-life. While everything was bare at the moment, he'd seen vids of what this place would look like when the weather patterns warmed. He wished he could get a chance to see it with his own eyes.

Earth's resources were astonishing. No wonder the planet had been given preservation status.

After some time, she stopped the car in front of a smaller dwelling than her own, but one with multiple outbuildings of varying sizes and shapes. One looked to be a hangar, like the one where she kept her car. Others were much smaller—barely big enough for someone to walk into and turn around.

There was little more than a shack with fencing around it, as if to keep something in. The fencing was weak enough that Serac didn't worry about what might be within the small building. He still made a mental note to monitor it.

"Here we are." She took a deep breath before opening her car door.

A refreshing breeze blew into the vehicle. Kimmy let out a small "eep" noise.

Serac joined her outside the vehicle. She was shivering already.

"You truly don't like the cold, do you?" he asked.

"Not so much—but I do like warming up afterwards." She glanced up at him, a small, furtive smile on her lips. That pink flush rose to her cheeks again, and she passed unnecessarily close to him as she headed for the dwelling.

Was it wishful thinking or was she expressing interest in him?

By the time they reached the door, it was already open. An older Earthling filled the entire space. He was even taller than Serac, which wasn't common, and was built with a similar musculature.

For a moment, Serac was reminded of his grandsire. He

had to hold himself back from slapping one hand to his chest in the standard greeting between Centauran warriors.

"Kimmy," the man said. "This is a nice surprise. Come on in, both of you."

Once again, Serac was being invited into someone's den. The man didn't even ask for a name.

Inside, Kimmy lingered close to Serac. She was still shivering. He'd never seen someone so affected by the cold before.

"I don't suppose we could have some cocoa, could we?" she asked.

The man chuckled. "Some things never change. Head on to the kitchen with your friend here."

The way he said *friend* put Serac's hackles up. His *zyln* sensed the challenge in the word, along with a bit of a threat.

The urge to respond to the challenge didn't come, though. Instead, Serac felt a need to earn the man's trust and acceptance.

Another sign of a mating bond.

Serac bowed his head slightly before following Kimmy into the kitchen. She grabbed a blanket from the back of the couch on her way, draping it over herself as she walked. Rather than sit next to her once they'd reached the room, Serac stood behind her chair.

"I'm Marvin, by the way." The man extended his hand as he joined them.

Serac knew this custom. He took Marvin's hand in his and shook it, noting how tightly the Earthling squeezed. He also stood very close to Serac, his gaze again filled with challenge.

"I am Serac."

The muscles along Marvin's jaw stood out as he clenched his teeth. His grip on Serac's hand increased to a point that was almost painful. But then, Marvin let out a sigh and released him.

"Both my girls," he muttered.

"Cocoa?" Kimmy prompted, in a small, plaintive voice.

"We must provide," his *zyln* thought.

Serac's gut lurched. "I will get it for you."

What was he doing? He didn't even know what cocoa was.

"I'll get it," Marvin said. "You just…stand there, I guess."

Marvin started opening cabinets and drawers, pulling out mugs, containers, a pan, and a bag of small, white… somethings. He filled the pan with milk—Serac remembered that from breakfast. He hoped Payback didn't plan to repeat his earlier behavior.

"So, what's on your mind?" Marvin asked while he continued his work.

"I… Um…" Kimmy stammered a bit, then looked up at Serac.

He rested his hand on her shoulder, giving her a

reassuring squeeze. She reached up and covered his hand with hers.

Walking into a plasma core must feel something like the sensations that passed through him at her touch. Every nerve in his body activated, like when he shifted, only so much better.

He might not have been able to help get her cocoa, but he could take the burden of the conversation from her.

"I requested an introduction," Serac said.

"This about the Scorpiian that's been harassing my girls?"

Serac was confused. Kimmy had referred to Marvin's grandchild as her friend, but Marvin spoke of them as if they were both his kin. And his demeanor toward her was definitely familial. Serac didn't need the heightened senses of his *zyln* to tell him that.

"It is," Serac said, putting aside his curiosity. "In part."

Kimmy frowned up at him. He hoped she didn't think he had deceived her—and yet, he hadn't been completely forthcoming in why he needed to see Marvin.

"I work for Hank," Serac said, pulling his gaze away from Kimmy to gauge Marvin's reaction.

The Earthling paused for a moment, then continued to stir whatever was in the pot. "And you can prove this, I suppose?"

"I can," Serac said.

Marvin turned around and leaned against the counter.

He crossed his arms over his massive chest. "Go ahead then."

Serac lifted Kimmy's hair from her shoulder. She sucked in a breath, her cheeks reddening. If Marvin hadn't been watching, Serac might have been tempted to brush his fingers along the pale skin he was revealing.

But Marvin *was* watching. So was Payback.

The parcel chittered angrily at Serac as he plucked him from Kimmy's shoulder. Serac held him up in one hand.

"Please tell me that isn't Payback," Marvin said.

The parcel's antennae perked up at the mention of his name.

Serac nodded. "It is."

Payback skittered back along Serac's arm, then jumped to Kimmy, burrowing into her hair. She rested her hand on the small creature briefly.

Marvin stepped forward, concern etched on his features. "He hasn't imprinted with her, has he?"

Serac glanced between the Earthlings, not sure what to say.

"I can take care of him," Kimmy said. "Taking care of animals is my job."

"Taking care of *Earth* animals is your job," Marvin said. "You have no idea what you're getting into here."

"Excuse me, but I think I do." Her tone had an edge of steel to it suddenly, a strength Serac hadn't heard before— except maybe while she'd been hitting the Scorpiian with a broom. "And besides," she said, "I've already gotten myself into it and there's no getting out of it even if I wanted to, which I don't, so it's settled."

Marvin let out a weary sigh as he turned back to the cocoa. He poured the liquid from the pan into three large mugs.

"It is far from settled," he said. "What do you think Hank is going to say when he finds out the parcel he meant for his sister has been hijacked by a human?"

"I..." Kimmy looked up at Serac, exuding worry so strong he felt it like a blow to the chest. "I didn't mean to. I don't want you to get in trouble."

"He won't," Marvin said. "Hank's sister is too young for a parcel, anyway. Hank probably sent Payback so soon because he doesn't approve of Craig and Barbara moving to Earth for their 'foster Earthling' and giving up their operation."

Marvin's relationship with Craig and Barbara was clearly well beyond professional. To be privy to that knowledge, they had to consider the Earthling a trusted friend.

"Wait, the same Lyrian named Craig that you introduced me to a few weeks ago?" She turned toward Serac. "He's your captain's dad?"

"He is," Serac said.

Marvin sprinkled some of the small, white, vaguely cubic items into the mugs, then brought two over to the table. He set one in front of Kimmy.

"Here you go, Buttercup," he said. "You never could stand the cold."

"Thanks." She wrapped her hands around the mug and leaned forward, inhaling the fumes from the liquid.

Marvin handed the other mug to Serac. It was giving off an amazing fragrance, and Serac's mouth started to water.

"I'm guessing Craig and Barbara's operation is the real reason your friend here wanted us to be introduced," Marvin said.

Every instinct in his body told Serac to be truthful with this man. Hank wanted to stake his claim on the smuggling routes out of Earth. Making contact with this level of a source was more than Serac had hoped.

But now that he was here, he wondered if he could go beyond that and actually make a delivery. If so, word would spread. It would go a long way toward establishing them as a legitimate source for illegitimate needs.

His mission was important.

So was Kimmy.

"We can keep her safe and *accomplish our goals,"* his *zyln* thought.

"How?"

"By keeping her with us."

Serac almost snorted. Of course, that was what his *zyln* wanted.

It was what he wanted, too.

"Continuing Craig and Barbara's operations is one of the reasons I wished to meet you," Serac said. "But you also need to know of the Scorpiian's continued presence in the area."

Marvin waved a dismissive hand. "I knew he hadn't left. Scorpiians don't back off when they think they're onto something of value."

"Mrs. Simpkins's cats?" Kimmy shook her head. "How can he possibly think they're valuable?"

Marvin stepped closer to Serac—a move he was sure was meant to intimidate.

"Because the Coalition still just sends people in to take what they want instead of asking," Marvin said. "They say they've changed, but I guess old habits die hard."

"Which is why we must keep the routes open," Serac said.

Marvin watched Serac closely. He knew he was being judged. He only hoped he was found worthy, for so many sentients' sakes.

Including his own.

Marvin smirked, then surprised Serac by reaching out and grasping his shoulder.

"I'll go get a shipment ready for you," Marvin said. "You can't do a smuggling run without something to smuggle."

Chapter Six

"Wait, smuggling?" Kimmy turned in her chair so she could face them both. "Is that the 'operation' you keep talking about?"

"How else is he supposed to get supplies to struggling planets?" Marvin asked.

"I don't know." Kimmy racked her brain for options. "Ask the Department of Homeworld Security for help?"

Serac shook his head. "They're doing what they can, but are being pulled in many directions at once. Our operation is still needed, and we can do the most good if we continue to work outside their scans."

"We say, 'under the radar' on Earth," Marvin said.

"Whatever you call it, it's wrong to go behind their backs," she said. "They're supposed to be running our interactions with aliens."

Marvin chuckled, then slapped Serac on the back and headed for the door. "I'm going to let you two sort this out."

The moment they were alone, Kimmy stood to face Serac, letting her blanket fall to the chair. She could feel Payback grab onto locks of her hair to keep his position at the nape of her neck. It was still a little weird having something constantly sitting on her shoulder.

"This isn't right," Kimmy said.

"Right?" Serac set down his cocoa, taking a step closer —and he had already been pretty close. "Many of the planets we help have been duped or pressured by the Coalition into giving away all the resources they need to sustain life. They have to live in domes on their own homeworlds. Others struggle to survive on the surface."

Kimmy had trouble wrapping her head around that. The only member of the Coalition she had met was Sabrina's new boyfriend, Len. He was Sadirian, and he was a sweetheart. A high-ranking sweetheart, if Kimmy understood correctly. He was Chief Science Officer of the *Reckoning*.

Though, now that she was thinking about it, that wasn't the friendliest name for a ship...

"I don't want to mess up this chance for Harbor to be a gathering place for aliens," she said. "We could make a difference for all of humanity. And maybe we can help the Coalition learn better manners, too."

The room felt colder than it had when they first arrived. Kimmy suppressed a shiver.

Serac reached down to grab the blanket, then draped it over her shoulders. He kept his hands resting there. Her body heated at his touch. Her brain might not know what to think of the situation, but the rest of her sure as heck knew how it felt about him.

"We won't prevent this opportunity for your town," Serac said. "I promise. My crew has been running our own smuggling operations for decades. Now that Craig and Barbara have given up their routes, someone needs to take over. Planets are depending on them."

"I've met Craig. He wouldn't leave people hanging."

"Hanging?"

Kimmy let out a sigh. "He wouldn't stop helping people if they needed him."

Serac nodded. "He has a new nestling to think about, plus his human foster-son. And if he's anything like my captain, Craig was probably counting on Hank stepping in to take over their role."

"It just…" She bit her lip and looked away, not wanting to offend him.

Serac cupped her cheek and brought her gaze back to his.

"What?" he asked. "You can tell me."

Her heart thumped, heat again spreading from his touch. Kimmy always did everything by the books. And this kind of activity sounded…not by the books.

She hoped saying so wouldn't put a permanent chill on their nascent relationship.

"On our planet, smuggling is illegal," she said. "But that would make you a criminal."

He nodded. "I am considered a criminal by the

Coalition and—"

He shut his mouth so hard and fast that his teeth clacked. This time, he was the one to look away—and she was the one reaching up to turn his gaze back to her.

"Then why are you doing it?" she asked, even though she already knew the answer.

"Because it's the right thing to do." He shook his head. "I can't risk going through *proper channels*, if such things actually exist now. We don't have that kind of time."

The skin around his eyes tightened and the furrows between his brow deepened. Something was there—a weight that she felt the strongest urge to ease.

How could she care so much when she didn't even know him?

But I feel like I do.

"One person can't save the world," she said. "And one planet can't save the galaxy."

He shook his head. "One person can do much more than they think, and when it comes to Earth, the potential is limitless."

"I don't understand how we can make such a difference. I mean, if there are as many planets out there needing help as you say, what's to stop us from becoming one of those barren worlds ourselves?"

He opened his mouth, then shut it again a few times. Finally, he sighed and cast a small smile at her.

Her stomach felt like it dropped through the floor. He

had finally smiled! And the way it softened his features…
It was so worth the wait.

"Let me show you," he said.

"Show me how?"

"Come with me. Help me make this delivery. Then tell
me what you think of our operation."

Was he offering to take her to outer space—to visit
another planet? How could she say no to that? And yet, if
what they were about to do was illegal… She didn't want
to end up in some space-jail.

"See with your own eyes," he said. "Make up your
mind on your own."

She did like the thought of that.

"What about Mrs. Simpkins's cats? Marvin said the
Scorpiian will keep going after them."

Serac shook his head. "Dean isn't just after Earth cats
anymore. He knows he can't handle them on his own."

"So, what is he after?"

"He's after you."

Chapter Seven

Kimmy stared at Serac for a few moments, her large eyes blinking behind her lenses. She didn't seem scared or concerned in the least.

Was there anything this beautiful Earthling feared?

"How do you know he's after me?" Kimmy asked.

In that moment, Serac himself was more afraid than he had perhaps ever been. The small omission of not telling her his main reason for visiting Marvin still sat like a weight within his chest. How could Serac not tell her the truth now?

She had expressed concern over him helping others by working outside the laws of the Coalition. What would she think of him when she learned of what he had done while working *within* those laws?

"Better to end this now. Let her know who I truly am," he thought.

"She will accept you."

Serac wished he shared his *zyln's* optimism.

"I know because he told me," Serac said. "It's the reason I came to Earth in the first place. Dean said he had found something of value and needed assistance obtaining it."

"Why did he think you would help?"

"Because we used to work together," Serac said. "I used to be one of the operatives who…who convinced sentients to give up their resources."

Her eyes narrowed. "So, you came here to kidnap me?"

"No," he said. "That life has been behind me for cycles. I came here to determine what he was planning and stop him if necessary."

"That's what you were fighting about in my backyard."

"Yes."

"And everything else you're doing, it's penance," she said. "You're trying to make up for the mistakes you made in the past."

"I…" He stammered a bit, amazed yet again at her insight into him. "I can never make it right, but I can make it better. I can try."

She hadn't pulled away, even with his revelation. If anything, she leaned closer to him. How could she be so trusting?

"I need to protect you," Serac said. They were the truest words he had ever uttered. "The safest thing is for you to come with me off the planet."

"If I go with you, it won't be because it's *safe*," Kimmy said. There was a strange edge to her tone. "I can handle this. I'm the youngest person to ever open a storefront in Harbor, and I'm killing it."

"You're…killing your store?" Serac asked.

She actually laughed a bit. "No, that means I'm doing an amazing job. My point is, I know how to take care of myself."

"But we will care for her now." Serac's *zyln* seemed just as confused as he was at her reaction.

"I have no doubt of that," Serac said. "At least, within your realm of experience—but Dean is well beyond that. I know him. I know what he's capable of."

Serac didn't want to think of what might happen to her if Dean captured her. Perhaps she was imagining it as well, because her brow furrowed and she frowned. Her gaze dropped from his.

She let out a burst of breath, then sat heavily, resting her elbows on her knees and covering her face with her hands. Serac wasn't sure what to do. All he knew was that he felt an irresistible urge to comfort her.

He knelt at her side—the offer of respect resonating through him as profoundly *right*—and gently touched her arm.

"Accepting assistance doesn't mean you're weak," he said.

"That's not it. I just… I didn't think you were offering to take me off the planet to keep me safe." She looked up at him and shrugged one shoulder. "I thought maybe you actually liked spending time with me as much as I like spending time with you."

His chest tightened and the hairs on his arms rose. She enjoyed his company?

"But of course you don't," she went on. "Sabrina's the only one who can stand being around my chatterbox self for any length of time, and now she's got Len, so I'm alone—well, except for Payback, and I know I can't keep him forev—"

Serac grasped her face and kissed her.

She let out a soft moan, leaning into him, parting her lips in invitation. He plunged into her mouth, savoring her taste, her warmth.

She wrapped her arms around his neck, pulling him closer. Her lips moved against his, her passion matching his own. Energy built within him, his skin tingling, every cell singing with life.

"Ahem." Marvin cleared his throat loudly behind them.

Serac broke off the kiss, but held Kimmy's gaze as he stood.

"I'm just going to put these in your car," Marvin said.

Fabric rustled by the door as Marvin headed outside. Serac barely noticed when the door opened and shut, except that Kimmy shivered from the chill breeze that blew in.

He lifted the blanket higher over her shoulders. Payback peeked his head out and scolded Serac, then burrowed into a more comfortable spot.

"Is he going to stay there all the time forever?" Kimmy

asked.

"No." Serac surprised himself by letting out a little laugh. "He just needs to get used to being imprinted to you."

Serac offered her his hand as she rose. They stood close, and the urge to kiss her again rose within him.

"Will you be all right in the cold?" he asked.

"Yeah." She looked down at their mugs of cocoa. "We shouldn't let these go to waste, though."

She picked up her mug and took a sip, then made an appreciative noise. Serac picked up his as well.

The scent was pleasing. He took a cautious sip and found it sweet and rich. The warmth of the drink seemed to spread out from his stomach. No wonder Kimmy liked it so much.

But she hates the cold...

The elemental spirits that Centaurans fused with gave them their immunity to cold, as well as the ability to change their shape. But it also made them radiate cold at times when they felt extreme emotions. He couldn't always control it.

Until she accepted his mate mark, she was vulnerable to his ability. He could hurt her.

"We will never hurt her," his *zyln* thought.

But she would still be uncomfortable because of his presence. The thought was unsettling.

"It's extra drafty in here today." Kimmy shivered again,

pulling the blanket closer.

Serac willed himself to calm. "We should take blankets along. My ship might be colder than you're used to."

And in the confined space, if he kept accidentally lowering the temperature, she would need them.

"Kimmy, I—" Before Serac could explain this aspect of his nature, the door opened again.

Marvin entered, bringing his own cold with him. He stomped to free his feet of snow.

"You're all loaded up," Marvin said. "This one's meant for Antares-3."

Antares-3 wasn't far—at least, not for Serac's ship. He was oddly disappointed.

He had hoped for more time alone with Kimmy.

The Antareans presented another issue for him. They would be able to sense what he was. He wasn't sure how they would react to a Centauran—even one bringing them vital resources for restoring their planet's ecosystem.

"My contacts on Antares-3 have worked with a private supplier from Earth before," Marvin continued, "though I hear she's part of the Department of Homeworld Security now."

"Well, Serac shouldn't keep them waiting." Kimmy took one more sip of her cocoa, then set down the mug.

"I thank you for the shipment." Serac pulled out a pouch filled with gold ore and handed it to Marvin. "I believe this mineral is considered valuable on Earth. We can provide it in abundance in exchange for more resources."

As Marvin emptied the pouch into his hand, Kimmy's eyes widened so much he could see the whites all the way around her irises. Her mouth dropped open and she stammered.

"Is that gold?" she asked.

Marvin shook his head, dumping the nuggets back in the pouch. He offered it to Serac.

"I don't need it," Marvin said. "That's not why I do this."

"Are you kidding me?" Kimmy's voice had reached a high pitch. She grabbed the pouch before Serac could take it. "We are so freaking investing this! I mean, selling it first, and then investing the money. You can fix up the farm, expand your house—"

"I have everything I need," Marvin said. "And your friend here probably has a schedule to keep, so we should argue later."

Kimmy scowled at him. "Fine. But I'm holding on to this in the meantime."

Serac extended his hand to Marvin in the Earth gesture. "You are a most excellent sentient."

Marvin shook it. "Just put the shipment to good use."

"And I will put *this* to good use." Kimmy shook the bag. "Once I have a better idea of this whole operation you have going, maybe I can find a way to legitimize it or something."

Marvin laughed and shook his head. "She's going to keep you busy," he said.

A shiver shot down Serac's spine. His body felt flooded with energy.

"He accepts us," his *zyln* thought.

There was no way the Earthling understood the significance of it, though. He didn't even know that Serac was Centauran.

Would Marvin still be as accepting if he knew that Serac's people were at war with the Coalition? It seemed impossible, but so much about his time on Earth had already surprised him.

Hope surged within Serac as he felt the bonding instinct grow stronger within him, the pull toward Kimmy intensifying. Now if only he could be sure that she felt the same.

Chapter Eight

The roads had been just as icy and slick on the way back to her house as they'd been traveling to Marvin's. For once, Kimmy was glad for it.

If she hadn't needed all of her focus on the road, her brain would have exhausted her with the questions spiraling in her head. The biggest being—*Was she nuts?*

Back at her house, she ran through the evidence against her sanity as she packed for the trip.

She'd just met this guy. He had admitted that he had come to Earth—because, oh right, he was an alien—answering a call from another alien who wanted to abduct her. He was considered a criminal in his society and had done even more ethically questionable things *before* becoming a criminal. And he wanted to take her to another planet.

And she wanted to go with him.

That was the crazy part. She *wanted* to be with him. Especially after that kiss.

She was still tingling all over from it. His lips had been cooler than she expected, and he tasted like mint. Seriously, like mint. It had been a stimulating and refreshing experience, which was…really unlike any kiss she'd ever had. But she loved it, chill and all.

He gave her shivers in the best possible way.

It was beyond physical, too. He shook her to her soul. She'd never felt so drawn to someone before.

I'll only be gone for a day. And a night…

She stuffed another sweater in her bag, wishing she had something slinky to take along.

"We should grab the blankets from the couch on the way out," Serac said. "If you can carry your gear, I can get the shipment from your transport."

"Transport?" She laughed. "Oh right. My car."

"Yes."

He seemed tense and distracted—eager to get underway. Serac had said he didn't want the people he was helping to have to wait. Maybe he had only kissed her earlier to get her to stop talking so they could move on.

No. No way could he kiss her like that and not mean it.

"I texted Sabrina so she knows to watch over the parlor till I'm back." Kimmy slung her bag over her shoulder— the one without the parcel on it—and headed out of her bedroom. "Do I need to bring along food or anything?"

"No. My ship can scan your physiology and determine what sort of nutrients you need. The food production unit will create nutrient bricks for you."

"How appetizing."

As they passed through the living room, she grabbed

the stack of blankets folded neatly on one of the cushions...exactly where she'd placed them the night before.

"Did you sleep last night?" she asked.

"I didn't require it," he said. "And I needed to remain alert and on guard."

"So, you just sat here awake all night."

"No, I stood outside your bedroom door."

"Oh."

Heat spread across her face and into...other more interesting areas at the thought. Only the thin panel of wood had separated them. If she'd known he was out there, she would have been tempted to invite him in. It would be easier to watch over her if he could actually see her, after all.

She started tingling all the way to her toes as she imagined what could have happened next. What could *still* happen next, depending on Serac.

Kimmy didn't consider herself to be impulsive when it came to bringing guys into her bedroom. Things were happening faster than she'd ever experienced. But then, she'd never met a guy like Serac.

On their way through the kitchen, she grabbed a box of cereal from the top of the fridge and put it on top of her stack of blankets.

He frowned deeply as he watched her. "I am capable of providing food for you."

Nutrient bricks did not sound appealing. She didn't want to hurt his feelings, though, so she said, "I know you can, but this is my favorite, and if we're going to be gone for a while, I might want some."

"Then I'll program my ship to be able to replicate it for you."

"Thanks."

She followed him outside and handed him the stack of blankets she was holding so she could lock her door. He carried it as they walked to her car, then gave it back once she'd popped the trunk.

Time to get a look at this precious cargo that was saving planets in need. Cargo that Serac had paid for *in gold*. She found she was holding her breath as he opened the trunk lid.

He lifted out a plastic tray sectioned into small compartments that were filled with dirt. A seed starter tray? There was a paper bag on top that actually had "Seeds" written on it.

Gardening supplies?

"That's it?" she asked. "That's what you're smuggling?"

"It is." Serac stared at the dirt in wonder for a moment, then slammed the trunk shut and headed toward the woods behind her house.

"Wait, you're going to all this trouble for *dirt* and..." She stared at the bag.

"Seeds," he said. "But it's so much more than dirt and seeds. It's hope."

"I really don't follow."

He stopped so suddenly that she ran into his back. His brow knit with worry as he turned.

"I thought you said you weren't following," he said.

She laughed and shook her head. "No, I meant your logic. I don't understand the significance."

"I'll explain on board," he said.

"Is your ship far?"

"It's right here." He took a few more steps, and the air in front of him shimmered. The shimmer coalesced into a sleek silver spaceship—in her own backyard.

"Oh my God," she said. "This has been in my yard the whole time?"

"It was cloaked."

"Still." She walked around the front of the ship to see more of it, for once not minding the cold.

There were two runners on the back of it, kind of like the metal feet on the bottom of a helicopter, but massive. Lights streaked along their length.

A sleek curve of metal rose up from them to form the rest of the ship which stood high above her head. Three poles stretched down from the front of the ship, ending in flat disks that sank a bit into the snow.

The ship itself had a bit of a "U" shape, with its sides stretched out like wings. There were windows at the top of it, and a hatch opened as she watched. A long ramp slid out of it, down toward the ground.

"This is so cool," she said.

"It's warmer inside."

She laughed. "No, cool means that something is awesome. This ship is awesome."

He cast a smile at her that she really wanted to see again. "Cool is a good thing, then? I'm glad."

It seemed a weird thing to say until she remembered that he came from an ice planet—and the strange, thrilling crispness of his kiss.

He gestured to the thin ramp.

I'm going on a trip in an actual alien spaceship.

She took a deep breath, and walked as quickly as she safely could, not wanting to give herself a chance to lose her nerve. When might she get another chance to go into space?

Okay, well, if Harbor did become a visitor's center for aliens, the opportunity might come up again, but this was her first time, and she was going into space with *Serac*. The trip was supposed to only take a day or two, but they'd be stuck together on the small ship.

Whatever could they do to pass the time?

Even though it was small, the inside of the ship was... cozy, in a chrome-and-plastic-looking-stuff sort of way.

The main color scheme was red and gray. To her left, a wall sectioned off the cockpit. A padded chair was centered behind windows and a semi-circle of control panels that lined the front of the ship. A low, padded bench ran across the middle wall of the cabin that sectioned off another room.

She peeked through the open archway and saw a fair-sized bunk built into the wall. Turning toward the hatch, she noticed another tiny room opposite the bunkroom.

"That's the bathroom, right?" she asked. She really hoped they were anatomically similar enough that his ship would have a bathroom.

He glanced over his shoulder to where she pointed. If this thing didn't have a bathroom, her plans for space travel were about to be derailed.

"That's the sanitation unit," he said. "Where bodily functions are—"

"That's good," she said. "Wouldn't want to ruin the mystery."

He knelt in front of the bench to set down the shipment of seeds and dirt, then hooked his fingertips under a panel in the flooring, lifting it. Dim, white light shimmered across the opening. He pressed a button and the light stopped.

The shipment fit pretty perfectly into what she guessed was a storage compartment. When he was done putting it in place, he reactivated the shimmery light, then put the floor panel back in place and stood.

"Smuggling compartment?" she asked.

"Stasis chamber. It will keep the shipment from being contaminated by anything we encounter on the way."

"Oh, oka— Wait, what now? What could we encounter?"

"Probably nothing. It's just a good idea to be prepared."

He pressed another control, this one on the wall near the hatch, and it closed, sealing them into the ship. Something in her expression must have given him pause, because he stepped closer.

"If you've changed your mind, we don't have to go," he said.

Kimmy shook her head. "No. I want to see what you do —how you help people."

He smiled. His amber skin darkened to a deep, rich gold. Was he blushing?

"I... You..." he began.

"Yes?"

"You can place your things in there." He gestured to the bedroom.

Tingling tendrils of sensation swept over her skin. He was looking at her so intently, she wondered if he was experiencing something similar. She felt her cheeks heat.

"Thanks," she said.

He followed her into the small space, then knelt next to the bed. At the tap of a flat panel near the foot of the bunk, a drawer opened. He opened another, and started quickly moving his belongings from the first, emptying it out.

Oh my God. Is he giving me a drawer in his place?

"You don't have to make space in your den for me."

She had been about to say something else, but stopped when he looked at her keenly, still kneeling on the floor. The intensity in his rich brown eyes left her speechless. *Her.*

"It is my honor to share my den with you," he said.

"Oh. Okay."

What a lame response!

But she was overwhelmed with a sense that this was something important. The room seemed to crackle with energy.

He stood—a lot closer than he had been before—and took the stack of blankets and the cereal box from her and placed them on the bunk.

"You can unpack your bag while I prepare for departure," he said. "If that's all right with you."

"That sounds great."

He bowed slightly, then exited the small space.

He wasn't far away. The ship was too small to let either of them really have space from each other. This would be a crucible to see if they really were compatible.

If he was even interested.

If *she* was interested.

Who am I kidding? I'm absolutely smitten.

It still didn't make sense, but wasn't that how it happened in her favorite books—the hero and heroine met and felt an instant connection?

She definitely felt a connection with Serac—and with the little guy stirring on her shoulder.

Payback ran down her arm, across her bag, and then jumped onto the pile of blankets on the bed, knocking them over. He used his six legs to good effect, quickly rumpling the blankets into a nest, then curled up in it and let out a cooing noise.

"I'm glad you're making yourself comfortable," she said. "Now if I can just settle in."

Chapter Nine

Serac listened to Kimmy speak to her parcel with growing tenderness. There was a female in his den. *Kimmy* was in his den.

His *zyln* flooded him with a contentment beyond anything he'd imagined.

He had never allowed anyone onto his ship before. Not even Hank—as if the Lyrian would fit in the space.

Serac wasn't sure how his captain would react to their family parcel imprinting with a human. He wasn't sure he cared. Payback had chosen Kimmy. Serac could see the appeal.

Brave, smart, caring, passionate, beautiful—she was everything he could have dreamt of in a mate. And she didn't mind that Serac was a shifter.

Of course, the fact that she was from an isolated planet like Earth probably helped with that. But she hadn't been afraid when he'd transformed right in front of her. That was beyond remarkable for someone who wasn't also a shifter.

"Werewolf," he murmured, keying in the command sequence that would take them into orbit.

"Space-werewolf," his *zyln* corrected.

Just because she seemed okay with what he was didn't mean she would want to bond with him. Neither did the fact that she'd seemed to enjoy it when they kissed.

When she had spoken of his ship as his den, he had wanted to rise and claim her right then. She had an instinctive understanding of Centauran nature that heated his blood.

He sensed her approach—the warmth she brought with her into the small command center of the ship. Schooling his expression, he turned the chair toward her.

"Where do you want me?" she asked.

He felt his eyes widen, knew that he was broadcasting...something. She smirked and stepped closer.

"I noticed there's only one chair," she said. "Is there someplace else I'm supposed to strap in?"

Serac cleared his throat. "This chair is the safest place in the ship during takeoff. But I need to be in it to handle the controls in case something goes wrong."

He was torn by the need to protect her, and the uncertainty of the best way to go about doing so.

Kimmy made the decision for him. She turned slightly, then sat on his lap.

"Problem solved," she said.

Perhaps that problem was solved, but a new one was growing and if she shifted her weight much at all, she was going to detect it.

Having her in his lap, in his arms, was too much of a temptation to pass up. He wrapped one arm around her waist, then spun the chair back toward the front of the ship. She let out a delighted squeal as he did so, the sound making his chest feel tight.

"I can't wait for this," she said.

His mouth went dry, his free hand dropping to her thigh. But when he looked to her, her gaze was locked out the front viewports.

Of course, she meant the take-off.

Swallowing down his disappointment, he said, "Then I won't delay."

He keyed in the command for departure.

The ship lifted smoothly from the ground, a ripple passing over the viewport to let him know the cloak had engaged. If he had thought of it, he would have slowed the speed of their departure to give her a chance to see and process more. He vowed to give her that experience upon their return.

A pale blue winter sky filled their view for only a few seconds, and then it thinned, revealing stars, and then the inky curtain of space.

"Oh wow." Kimmy leaned against his chest, her heart beating hard enough for him to feel it. He tightened his embrace.

"This is just... It's amazing." She reached up and swiped a trembling thumb across her cheek.

He caught her hand before she could wipe the tear from her skin, bringing it to his lips to kiss. She turned toward him, lips parted, then pressed her mouth to his.

He held himself still at first, letting her explore him, opening his mouth at her gentle prompting. But then, he could hold back no longer.

He grasped her face in his hands, angling her head to get better access, to thrust his tongue deeper into the soft heat of her mouth. She let out a soft moan, spurring him on.

He leaned forward in his chair, only then realizing he hadn't even secured the safety harness. At the moment, he didn't care.

They needed a horizontal surface. Stars, they needed any surface he could hold her against without being in danger of pressing the wrong command panel.

He spun the chair back toward the main cabin of the ship. He could carry her to his bunk, lay her among her blankets, press himself into her, and place his mark upon her.

No.

He pulled back from the fantasy.

Bonding among Centaurans was permanent. She was an Earthling and had no idea of what she'd be getting into, even if she was interested.

He broke off the kiss. "Kimmy, this isn't something we should do."

"Oh."

He hated the way her face dimmed, desire turning to disappointment. And he hated himself for causing her even that pain.

"I'm sorry," she said. "Wait...no, I'm not sorry. You're as into this as me. Unless you *don't* actually like spending time with me. Probably because I talk too much. But still, you shouldn't—"

He cupped her cheek in his hand and leaned in to kiss her again, not letting up until he felt her relax against him. When she had, he once again forced himself to stop.

Still close, breaths mingling, he said, "I enjoy your presence immensely. Especially the talking parts."

Her lips curled up in a smile. "Not the kissing parts?"

He actually chuckled. "Those, too. But there are things about me that you don't understand."

"What kind of things? I mean, I get that you're an alien. And a werewolf. And a smuggler, but a good-guy one." She arched an eyebrow. "Or so you say."

Her tone was playful enough to elicit yet another laugh. How could she break through his walls so easily? He couldn't remember the last time he'd smiled before meeting her, and now, it felt as if he constantly was.

"I need to explain some things about...kissing," he said. "And what it can lead to."

She leaned in closer. "More kissing?"

That time, he let out a full laugh.

"Are we—" her cheeks turned bright pink, "physically compatible?"

A thrill shot through him at the thought of how absolutely compatible their bodies were, and how he would love nothing more than to show her. He took advantage of her closeness for yet one more kiss. Hopefully, not the last.

Just in case, he took his time, tasting her, savoring everything about the experience. The way she melted into him pushed the limits of his restraint. She didn't hold any part of herself back. He wanted to do the same.

"We are compatible," he said. "But if we move forward with this… I don't know if I can control myself."

She swallowed hard. He traced the delicate line of her neck with his fingertips, and she shivered.

"You think you'll hurt me?" she asked.

"What? No. Never. I could never hurt you."

"Then what?"

He looked away, but she grasped his cheek and made him face her.

"What is it you're afraid of?" she asked.

"I want… I need…" He took a deep breath and blew it out. "I feel an urge to put my mark on you."

"Oh, wow." Her eyes widened, and she got that far-off look that he hadn't quite figured out yet. It was almost as if she was seeing through him.

"And you're afraid that if we do…more than kissing,

you'll mark me as yours?" she asked.

She seemed to have a remarkable grasp on the situation. Still, he shouldn't assume.

"Cen..." He almost said, "Centaurans," but stopped himself.

Vapor pits. If he truly wanted to mate with her, he should just tell her and get it over with.

"We mate for life," he said.

"And you want me to be your mate. You feel drawn to me—connected in a way you never have before."

His jaw dropped open. "Yes. How did you know?"

How could she understand him so well after so short a time?

"I've read hundreds of werewolf romance stories," she said. "They're my favorite."

Her cheeks pinked up again.

Serac stilled. Did she actually like him as an individual at all, or was she just fascinated by his shifter nature? The High Council had been intrigued by Centaurans and it had led to tragedy.

Yet with the strength of the instinct driving him to claim her, did it matter why she was drawn to him?

He shook the thought away. It *did* matter.

He wouldn't mate with someone who saw him as a curiosity.

Chapter Ten

"I should monitor our drop into blue space."

Serac's tone chilled, along with the air in the small cockpit. Kimmy shivered, wishing she had left her jacket on.

He wasn't looking at her—and worse, he'd stopped touching her. What had she said that had offended him so badly?

It wasn't the first time she'd totally killed the mood with her chattering, but with Serac, she had thought things were different. That he accepted her—even liked her talking. Heck, *he had just said* that he liked her talking. So what had changed?

She slid from his lap, but hovered in the opening between the cockpit and cabin. The silence started to freak her out, especially as she thought about the emptiness surrounding them.

Unable to stand the quiet any longer, she said, "What's blue space?"

He paused for long enough that she wasn't sure he would answer. As it was, he kept working on the controls and didn't turn to face her.

"It's the fabric that holds our universe together. It underlies everything," he said. "Blue space runs just beneath or above or to the side of our reality—however you wish to view it. When we enter it, we can travel enormous distances in relatively short periods of time."

"Cool." She wished she had something more erudite to say, but she was still stung by his sudden rejection.

"We won't reach our destination for several hours. Perhaps you should rest."

Wow, a rejection and *a dismissal.*

She didn't bother responding. It was getting so cold in the cabin, she just wanted to wrap up in all her blankets and take a pity nap.

She hurried back to the bedroom and pulled her jacket on, then sat on the bunk as far from the door—and Serac—as she could. It was still freezing. She lifted the top blanket. Payback came with it, chittering angrily.

"Not you, too," she said.

Payback's pink fur—and glow—darkened to purple and then a somber blue. He ran over to her and rested three of his legs on her thigh, his antennae pointing at her as he squeaked.

"I'm sorry I disturbed you." She sniffed, telling herself it was from the cold, and not the cold shoulder she'd just received.

She grabbed more blankets and pulled them around her, curling up on the bunk and hugging her knees. Payback climbed up to stand on them, putting him at eye level. He let out a squeak that sounded uncannily like a question.

"I'm okay," she said.

Now she was lying to the parcel as well as herself. Payback tilted his head.

She raised her voice enough that she was sure Serac could hear her. "I know you guys are from ice planets, but could you maybe make it a little warmer in here?"

Payback turned toward the door and started chittering angrily. His fur turned bright red and let off a stronger glow.

"I can insulate the bunk room and maintain the temperature at a more comfortable level for you." Yet again, Serac spoke from the cockpit. He didn't even lean back so she could see him.

The door slid shut.

For a moment, her heart seemed to stop. Was he trapping her in here? Was he abducting her? Had this been part of his plot all along?

For all she knew, he was taking her to Dean. He had admitted the pair used to work together.

But no. No. She was being ridiculous.

Just because something had passed between them that had…negated the other, much more pleasant stuff that had passed between them, it didn't mean Serac was a bad guy. She refused to believe her judgment was that far off.

She brooded in his room for what felt like a long time,

her thoughts fading into a dream as she fell asleep.

Something soft and furry woke her up, wriggling against her neck. Had she fallen asleep at the office again? Except, the office didn't have a metal ceiling.

Wait, metal ceiling?

She sat up quickly, trying to get her bearings through the just-waking-up-fog. Everything was unfamiliar. The furry thing clung to her neck with way too many legs. She peeled it off of her and held it up where she could see.

Bright pink fur. Huge eyes. Antennae.

"Squee?" it said.

She yelped and dropped it on the bed, struggling to untangle herself from the blankets and falling toward the floor. Somebody caught her right before she hit the hard surface.

"Serac?" Her mind cleared as she looked into his rich amber eyes.

"Are you all right?" he asked.

The angry chittering coming from beneath the blankets on the bunk helped bring her further back into the moment and her new reality. She was on a spaceship heading for another planet with a guy who ran volcano-hot, then glacier-cold.

And who was also a werewolf.

And she'd just offended her new pet parcel.

"I'm sorry, Payback," she said, pushing away from Serac's chest. She dropped to her knees by the bed so that she was on eye level with the parcel. "I'm bleary when I wake up."

She reached into the blankets and pulled Payback out. He was flashing between bright red and yellow, his fur standing on end.

"Oh, little guy," she said. "I really am sorry."

As she stroked the parcel, he gradually stopped squeaking at her, his fur flattening and turning pink again. The glow subsided as well.

"Still friends?" she asked.

Payback let out a disgruntled squeak, then climbed up her arm and snuggled against her neck again.

"I guess that's a yes." She laughed, relieved that she'd been forgiven.

Serac had moved next to the open door and was watching her silently.

"What about us?" she asked, quietly. "Are we still friends?"

His eyebrows rose and he actually stepped back a pace. "I... I didn't know we were."

"Well, I don't normally fly off into space with people I don't like. I thought..." She shook her head. "You said you liked me, too. You certainly acted like it."

"I did," he said. "I do."

He sighed, then walked into the room and sat at the foot of the bunk, resting his elbows on his knees. The space wasn't all that big, and he took up much of it. Still, she didn't feel threatened by his presence. Rather, she was reassured by it.

She sat next to him, giving him a little distance, but not too much. It was a balance she was used to striking—close enough to let someone know she was there for them, but not so close that they felt smothered. She waited for him to speak, forcing herself to be okay with the silence for once.

"I haven't been as open with you as you have been with me," he said. "There are things I should tell you—aspects of who and what I am that I need you to know."

"Then just tell me. Anything is better than how you suddenly started ignoring me."

"I didn't mean to." His spine stiffened as he reached for her. But he quickly pulled back, clenching his hands into fists and returning them to his lap. "I wish more than anything to be close to you and I don't know how to handle that. If I caused you distress, I am truly sorry."

She smiled. "I accept your apology. Just don't do it again. If you have something I need to know, we can talk it out." She gently bumped her shoulder against his. "I think you've figured out by now how much I love to talk."

He nodded and even laughed softly. After a few moments of silence, he spoke again.

"I...am...Centauran." It took effort for him to get out each word. He looked up at her, lips parted, eyes pinched, as if he was expecting something bad.

"Okay," Kimmy said.

"Did they not tell you? Do you not know?"

"Know what?"

"The Tau Centauran Assembly. The sentients who are at war with the Coalition. My people are the driving force behind it."

"Oh." She remembered Len and Marvin talking about it.

But Earth was being left out of the war. At least, for the moment. And they had the Vegans—who were apparently bad-ass, super-tech-powered lizard-people—on their side.

"I'm sorry to hear that," Kimmy said. "But just because your people are fighting with...I guess my people's friends, that doesn't mean we have to be enemies. Does it?"

"Most sentients think that it does."

"Why?"

"Because Centaurans are extremely loyal to our clans, to our people. And my people want vengeance for the terrible things the Coalition has done."

She remembered Marvin talking about that, too. Len hadn't denied any of it. He just kept saying that they had changed.

"I thought it was the High Council that had done the terrible things," Kimmy said. "And they're gone now."

"They may be gone, but the people who followed those orders are not and we can't be sure that everyone who was sympathetic to them has been neutralized."

"Neutralized?" Her voice rose to a tiny squeak.

"Not like that," he said. "Not in all cases, anyway. I mean removed from positions of power. It's hard for Centaurans to trust others, especially with how our trust was betrayed when we were first brought into the Coalition of Planets."

Kimmy reached for his hand. She held it in both of hers, resting them on his thigh.

He took a deep breath and let it out slowly. The room grew cold again. She scooted closer to him, but that only seemed to make it worse.

"Let me get you a blanket," she said.

He held tight when she tried to pull her hands away.

"It won't help," he said. "The cold is coming from me."

She felt her eyebrows rise. "You have cold powers *and* you're a shifter? Wow."

That time, he was the one to pull away. He clamped his hands together in front of him.

"I can't always control it," he said. "It's an automatic defense mechanism."

Defense mechanism? Did that mean he felt threatened by her? The idea was ludicrous. And yet...

"Centaurans are structurally and genetically similar to Sadirians," Serac said. "Similar enough that the High Council took a very keen interest in trying to understand and replicate what we can do."

Kimmy tried to keep her voice gentle. "I'm guessing

they weren't very nice about it."

"They started by initiating mating bonds with Centaurans," he said. "Like Earthlings, Sadirians are close enough biologically that the mating instinct can be triggered with the right person."

His cheeks darkened and he looked away. For a moment, Kimmy wondered if maybe *she* had triggered that response in *him*. If they were meant to be together, it would explain the incredible kisses and the instant attraction she'd felt.

"Let me guess," she said. "They did that so the Centaurans would feel loyal to the Coalition and would go along with what the High Council wanted."

His mouth dropped open, then closed. He shook his head.

"Yet again, you hold an understanding of my people that amazes me," he said. "I must read some of those paranormal romance novels you've been talking about."

"When we get back to Earth, you can borrow whatever you like."

And after he read the books, he'd have to return them. She'd be sure to loan him more every time to keep that going. The idea of him walking out of her life when this was all over was not something she could face at the moment.

She scooted closer and rested her arm on his back gently. There was more to the story. She could sense it, but she didn't want to push.

"The High Council created situations where many Centaurans and Sadirians were together, trying to trigger mating bonds," he said. "And when we bonded with them, some of our abilities transferred to our new mates. They couldn't shift or generate cold, but mated pairs could sense each other's emotions. Our Sadirian mates became immune to the temperature changes we can create—and to all cold."

For the first time ever, she saw him shiver. Now she knew it definitely wasn't because of the temperature.

His voice became gravelly as he went on. "The High Council became focused on trying to find a way to extract the source of that change. They wanted to see if they could genetically engineer Sadirians who could survive the cold of space, even without a uniform."

Kimmy did not like where this was going. "So, they experimented on you."

Serac nodded. "And our mates. Those who had been recruited tried to explain that the ability wasn't something that could be replicated, but the High Council wouldn't listen. They also wouldn't stop."

"That's awful."

"Few of the Sadirians survived. Centaurans mate for life, and when our mates die, so do we."

The temperature in the room dropped at least another ten degrees. Kimmy started to shiver. She couldn't help it.

"I apologize." Serac reached for the blankets and draped them around her. "I shouldn't be thinking of this, let alone telling you."

"It's okay," she said. "I want to know."

He nodded. "It is wise to know your enemy."

"What? No. You're not my enemy." She reached out of her burrow of blankets to hold his hand again. "I want to know because I want to know more about *you*. Who you are and what you've been through. What makes you... Serac."

Some of the tension eased from his expression.

"You should know that I've been exiled," he said.

She gasped, the implications of that running through her mind. She knew a lot of her reactions were coming from what she'd read in books, but so far, they seemed to be spot on, and the idea of a werewolf being kicked out of his pack was awful.

"I'm so sorry," she said. "That must be terrible for you."

"The High Council has been destroyed. My people have had their revenge. Yet they insist on pursuing their war, letting the Tau Ceti urge them on."

Len had called the Tau Ceti "vampire space frogs." She was glad she'd encountered the space version of a werewolf first.

"Centaurans have a source for...advanced technology. I can't tell you more than that. But the Tau Ceti carry the bloodlust in their hearts. This ship was an early prototype of a scouting vessel capable of entering blue space without a drop gate. No one has ever been able to achieve that technology in a ship this small."

He was quiet for a moment, then said, "If the Assembly could mass produce ships like this, they would be able to reach every corner of the galaxy. Sentients would be at their mercy. But the Tau Ceti are even worse than the High Council in many ways. They have *no* mercy."

"Then how can you be allied with them?"

"I can't." He spoke more quickly as he went on, as if he was afraid something would keep him from continuing. "I stole this vessel and destroyed all of the records regarding its creation. It set us back decades. Enough time, I hope, for this conflict to be resolved peacefully."

The despair in his expression left little doubt in her about his fate.

"But you won't be able to go back," she said. "Even then."

He let out a slight chuckle—the saddest laughter she'd ever heard.

"Yet again, you know us so well," he said. "No, they won't accept me again. I've betrayed my people in their eyes. I will not be welcome on my homeworld again."

"I get it now," Kimmy said. "After you left Dean, you lost your home trying to help others and now you've dedicated yourself to helping people save theirs."

His features smoothed further. He looked away and shook his head.

"It's so hard to believe," he said, "that I could have found someone who understands me so well."

She squeezed his hand tighter. "Trust is hard to give when you've been around so much betrayal. But I won't betray you. I promise."

Chapter Eleven

Serac's chest tightened. He wanted to believe her. Every cell in his body told him to trust.

She had listened to him so earnestly, without judgment. Maybe he was wrong about why she was interested in him. Maybe she saw him as something more than just a shifter.

"Claim her," his *zyln* urged.

He reached out and cupped her cheek, leaning in to kiss her. She met him half-way, wrapping her arms around his neck.

Her lips were so warm. He had to be freezing her, but when he tried to pull away, she held on tighter, opening her mouth to him. He plunged in at the invitation, pressing her back on the bunk.

She slid her leg along his, latching on to his thigh and pulling him closer. The blankets had fallen away, and only the thin layers of their clothing separated them.

Her neck was bare to him. He kissed his way to her nape, her gasps spurring him on.

"Hold on," she said.

She reached up under her hair and pulled out Payback. He chittered at them angrily, his fur turning a vibrant green that Serac had never seen from the creature. Then the parcel scurried to the side of the bunk and leaped to the floor, dragging one of the smaller blankets behind him. He was still making angry squeaks as the blanket disappeared out the door.

Serac and Kimmy looked back at each other for a moment, then both burst into laughter. He couldn't remember ever laughing like that—not in his entire life.

But her smile, her gaze, her warmth... It flooded him. Changed him. Made him want to be more for her.

Made him want more *from* her.

"I wish for us to bond." He regretted the confession almost immediately. It was much too soon to be asking for something like that.

Kimmy reached up to stroke his cheek. "I know it's crazy, but I want that, too."

He wasn't sure he'd heard her correctly—couldn't believe his senses. Part of him didn't want to push, but he had to be certain. "Because I'm one of these werewolves you like so much?"

"Of course not. Because you're you, and what I feel for you, the pull... It doesn't make sense. It's sudden and it's strong."

She was describing a mating bond, and if she shared the instinctive attraction, he knew it was real.

"That is the way with Centauran bonds," he said.

"That is the way with a lot of the stories I read. I just

never actually thought I'd be living one. I dreamed about it, but this is so much better than anything I imagined. You are better than anything I imagined."

His skin pebbled as longing washed over him—filled him with need and something stronger. No one had ever spoken to him like that.

"The truth about our nature—"

She shook her head. "You don't have to tell me."

"You need to know."

He took a deep breath, preparing to tell her the greatest secret of his people—one only shared with mates from other worlds.

"Centaurans are not a singular life-form," he said. "When we are born, the links to our parents and kin keep us safe from the cold, but when we come of age, we take on an elemental spirit. We call them *zyln*. They are what give us our ability to survive and generate cold, as well as our shifting abilities."

"Oh wow." Her gaze became unfocused for a moment, then she nodded. "I've read stories like that."

How fortunate could one sentient be?

She laughed. "I thought I was just reading for fun. I had no idea I was actually learning about my soulmate."

"Soulmate…"

Her cheeks turned pink. "It means that we're destined to be together. We feel like we've known each other forever because our souls know and…and love each other already."

His *zyln* rumbled in approval of the word. Mated souls. It was a lovely—and apt—concept.

"You are beyond my greatest dream," he said.

He kissed her again, burning every sensation into his memory. The way her hands felt pulling on the fabric of his shirt, the lingering taste of cocoa on her lips.

He leaned back to pull his shirt off and toss it aside. Her eyes widened, and she hissed in a breath.

"Wow, you're gorgeous," she said, dusting her fingertips over his chest.

"And you are beautiful," he said. "Exquisitely so."

"I... Thanks." She blushed again.

"Has no one ever told you that before?"

She shook her head.

"Then you've been surrounded by fools."

She blushed deeper as she glanced up at him, running her hands down along his abs. When she reached his jeans, she started working the fastener.

His dick was so hard, begging to be touched. What would it be like to be touched by his mate? To feel her hands wrap around him? To plunge himself into her heat?

He didn't have to wait long to find out.

She slid her hand past the waistband of his undergarment as soon as she'd opened his jeans, fingers circling his shaft. Sensation jolted through him, knocking the breath from his lungs. He reached out to brace his arms on the walls in the corner of the room to keep himself upright.

"Kimmy."

"We need to be naked," she said. "Like, now."

She released him, then scooted herself up in the bunk. It took him a moment to shake himself from the lust rising up in him. He stifled a growl as she slipped from the bunk.

It helped when he turned to see her throwing her jacket on the floor, then practically tearing her sweater from her body. Her glasses almost went with it.

"That wasn't very graceful," she said. "I'd take them off, but honestly, I want to be able to see absolutely everything with you."

"Then you shall."

He turned to sit on the side of the bunk, quickly removing his boots and socks. By the time he was done with that task, Kimmy had taken off most of her clothing. Apparently, it was easier to remove.

She was only wearing undergarments. He'd never seen anything like them, though. A small scrap of fabric was wrapped around her torso and held up with straps. The material had a transparent pattern and barely covered her small breasts.

He wanted to take the soft mounds in his lips. His mouth watered at the thought.

"Naked," she said, slapping her hands together. "Now."

He laughed as he rose. "I can deny you nothing."

"I really like the sound of that."

He hooked his fingers on the waistbands of both his jeans and undergarment and slid them down, kicking both off at once.

Kimmy's jaw dropped and her eyebrows hiked up her forehead. Her glasses were a bit askew on her face.

"Oh...wow...that's..." She cleared her throat as she stared at his dick.

He felt a ripple of sensation across his back as he took in her appraising—and approving—look. His hands flexed with the need to hold her, to pleasure her, to claim her.

"Okay, so I'm glad that's quite like what I'm used to," she said. "But we'll definitely need to be sure my body is ready for...you know."

He didn't know. Did she mean children?

The idea of starting a family with her was... overwhelming. He couldn't even name all of the emotions that rose within him at the thought.

"Our bond will need to strengthen for at least one of your solar years before your body will be ready to bear my children," he said. "Nothing will happen in that regard until then."

Her eyes widened and her mouth dropped open. "I meant ready to accommodate your hugeness."

"Oh."

Of course that's what she meant. And now he had most likely scared her away by bringing up such an important topic so soon.

"But that's really good to know." She smiled at him, and said, "A year seems like a good amount of time to settle in together before we take that step."

Was she still interested in proceeding? He barely dared to hope, and yet, she wasn't moving away.

She reached behind herself and undid some sort of clasp, letting the scrap of fabric around her chest fall to the ground. Her last undergarment joined it, leaving her naked before him. She stepped closer, resting her hands on his chest.

He hadn't scared her off. Still, he had to be sure she hadn't changed her mind.

He wanted to ask, but all that came out when he tried to speak was, "Mine."

She nodded, her voice breathless as she responded. "Yours."

That was all he needed—all he could stand.

He grabbed her and spun them both around, their inertia taking them onto the bunk. Before they hit the bed, he caught his weight on his elbows to keep from crushing her.

He captured her lips with his, his tongue demanding entry. She welcomed him, her arms tight around his back. She slid one of her legs up his, pulling him closer. He doubted her body was ready for him, though.

He grasped her leg and pushed it back on the bunk, pinning it in place with his thigh. With his hand already close, he reached for the softest folds of her skin.

She gasped at the initial contact, back arching toward him. He growled his approval against her mouth. As he thrust his fingers into her slick heat, he deepened the kiss.

Her hips moved against his hand, and the plaintive notes of need she made nearly drove him crazy. But he waited until he was sure she was ready before positioning himself at her core.

His energy shifted within him, coiling in a way that was new. He broke off the kiss to look into her eyes.

"Mate," he said.

"Mate," she whispered back.

Chapter Twelve

The moment the word left her lips, Serac plunged into her. Her core stretched to welcome him, gripping tight. She was really glad he'd prepared her body for him.

He hadn't prepared her for the cold.

It radiated out from him, rolling along her skin like fog. She should be shivering, but all she felt from it was... pleasure. The cold was like a caress, sweeping over her skin.

He let out a groan, holding still for a few moments. When he started to move his hips, she felt it like the ebb and flow of the tide. Each stroke reverberated through her nerve-endings, lighting her up with a white-hot energy like fire and lightning combined.

The feeling intensified along with his thrusts, crashing through her. She wrapped her legs around his waist, raked her nails down his back. He reached for her arms and pulled her hands up next to her head, interlacing their fingers.

Her heart was beating so fast it almost hurt. She could feel Serac's racing in time with hers. She could feel...

She could feel him on the edge of her senses—a light, a

warmth, a feeling of longing and welcoming and blossoming love.

She let herself fall toward him, wanting all of that and more. Wanting to give him everything.

Serac leaned back, his eyes blazing white. A softer glow emanated from both of their bodies, shining in the center of their chests. The light streamed out between their hearts, pulsing with each beat, a tether that grew brighter with each thrust.

Goosebumps rose across her skin everywhere. Her entire body tingled, charged with an energy that went beyond the physical pleasure he gave her. She felt it coil deep in her belly, then burst free, soul-deep ecstasy flooding through her.

Serac clenched his eyes shut, light still escaping along the seam of his lids. His thrusts grew frenzied, taking her higher as she pulsed around him, pulling everything she could from him as he spilled himself in her.

He thrust deep and held there, exhaling puffs of fog. All around them, tiny slivers of ice hung suspended in the air. She took a deep breath and let it out slowly, watching as it joined with his. She should be freezing, but she felt perfectly warm.

"That was so…" She smiled. "Cool."

He chuckled, then kissed her again, this one much more tender. He rolled off of her, but kept his arms around her and held her close.

Was it done? She could only remember him kissing her neck. Still, she felt…different. Her body was energized and the air on her skin seemed to have lost its chill, even though she could see frost on the walls.

The link she had felt to Serac was muted. She could still sense a steady contentment and happiness coming from him.

"What is it?" he asked.

His eyes were closed and she hadn't said anything. Maybe he was sensing her emotions as well.

"In my books, the mate mark is given through a bite," she said.

"A bite?" He shook his head. "I would never bite you."

"Then how am I marked?"

He laughed, then propped himself up on his elbow. Gesturing to his neck with his other hand, he pointed out a small, silver crescent-shape at his nape. She hadn't noticed it before.

"Only a bonded pair shows this mark," he said. "And each pair's mark is subtlety different from all others."

"I have one, too?"

"Yes. An identical match to mine."

She wanted to run to the nearest mirror and look at it, but then he traced his fingertips over her neck in the same spot. Goosebumps rose on her skin, desire spiking at his touch. He let out an unsteady breath, then leaned down and kissed her.

His longing flowed through her, amplifying her own, feeding from it. She clutched at his back, drawing him closer.

A persistent beeping broke into the moment.

Serac pulled away and sighed. "We're almost to the exit point."

"Darn."

"But we'll have the trip back to Earth," he said.

"And the rest of our lives after that."

Excitement and nervousness fought within her. She hoped he couldn't feel the second part. Everything had happened so quickly between them.

She saw his eyebrows furrow and reached up to trace the lines, easing them away. Quick didn't mean it was wrong.

"This is the beginning of our greatest adventure," she said.

He grasped her hand and kissed it.

The beeping grew in volume. Serac sighed, then nimbly rolled off the bunk to his feet.

"I have to prep the ship to return from blue space." He gathered up his clothes and started to dress.

Kimmy still couldn't believe how comfortable she was lying naked in a cold ship. It seemed like a good idea to put on some clothes as well, though.

Moving as fast as she could, she managed to get dressed at about the same time as he did. It helped that he stopped to watch her several times.

"Liking the show?" she asked.

"Enjoying the glimpse of my future."

"Wow, you really know just what to say."

He took her hand in his and led her to the cockpit. Kimmy glanced around the main cabin and saw that Payback had pulled the blanket he'd run off with up onto the bench and formed a small nest with it. She could just see his antennae sticking out.

This was her new family. She felt like she should be panicking at the sudden commitments, but all she felt was happiness. That was quickly overpowered by awe as Serac sat in the main chair and pulled her into his lap.

The windshield—or whatever it was called on a spaceship—was completely filled with swirls and eddies of blue. The background was pure cobalt, like her grandma's favorite glasses. Streaks of indigo and crackling lightning-teal sped past them. It was beautiful and terrifying.

"Are you sure your ship can handle this?" she asked.

Serac laughed. "I wouldn't have brought you aboard otherwise."

He managed to key in controls by reaching around her, rotating the chair as he needed. Even with all the unknowns, being in his arms made her feel safe. She relaxed against his chest, letting the feeling fill her.

He took in a deep breath and let it out, pausing in what

he was doing to hold her in his arms. "And I thought making love with you was the best thing I'd ever feel."

She laughed, and when she lifted her face to his, he captured it in his hands and kissed her. She rose to kiss him back better, climbing up his lap so she could straddle him in the seat.

His hands went to her ass, crushing her against him. He wanted her so bad, she could feel it in every cell—and she wanted him just as much.

The controls started beeping again.

Kimmy laughed against his lips, delighted to feel his smile, inside and out. She could absolutely get used to this.

Serac picked her up and set her back across his lap, growling under his breath. He reached across her and struck a panel harder than seemed wise.

The blue around them shimmered, then paused. A moment later, it winked to black. Slowly, stars bled back into their view. She could barely see a pale orange planet in the distance.

"Is that where we're going?" she asked.

"Yes."

"Then let's get this mission done so we can celebrate."

Serac chuckled. "Agreed."

The planet was already growing closer. Her nerves were growing as well.

What would the people of Antares-3 be like? What would they think of her?

The name sounded familiar. She thought perhaps Len and Sabrina had mentioned it. Kimmy wished she had paid more attention. She had still been getting used to the whole "aliens are real" thing.

Sitting in Serac's lap, she was glad to have had at least that part of meeting him squared away before everything that had passed between them.

What if this was what her life was going to be like? She could already tell that she wouldn't want to be away from Serac, but she also had her pet parlor to run. How would they manage everything?

They probably should have talked about this before mating. Still, she couldn't bring herself to regret anything. She knew they would work it out.

"Ask," he said.

"Ask what?"

"The questions roiling inside you. Ask."

She took a deep breath, then said, "How are we going to make this work? I have a business on Earth. You have a business in space."

"You are my priority," he said. "If our relations with Earth grow as I hope, my captain will need someone planetside to oversee his operations. He'll lose me as his scout, but I believe he'll keep me on in that capacity rather than lose me all together."

"You would give up what you do for me?"

"It isn't a sacrifice. It's a gift." He was quiet for a

moment, but the longing within him spoke to her loud and clear. "I've been wandering the galaxy for so long that I barely remember what it's like to have a homeworld. If you're willing, I would love to make Earth my home."

She smiled at him. "I would love that, too."

Chapter Thirteen

Too many emotions were vying for control. Serac had bonded with Kimmy. She had accepted him into her life, her home, her heart. They were joined permanently. His isolation was over.

It was still hard to believe.

"Mate. Den. Home." His *zyln* kept chanting the words in his mind, as if it was having as much trouble believing their good fortune as Serac himself.

"Tell me more of what your people expect from me," he said. "Apparently, your stories didn't get everything right. What do they think of werewolves?"

"For one thing, they don't think werewolves are real," she said. "But then, most people don't think aliens are real, either."

"If they did believe, what would they think?"

"Well, a lot of our stories say you can't control when you change form and that you have to change on the full moon. And that silver can kill you."

"If it's formed into a strong enough weapon, I suppose it can. Is that why you mentioned silver after running at Dean with a broom?"

"Yeah."

His stomach clenched as he remembered her rushing into battle with only that flimsy weapon. Taking on a Scorpiian with a stick.

"Our mate is fierce," his *zyln* thought.

And perhaps a bit too impulsive. Serac didn't wish her to change anything about herself, though. She followed her heart. Her heart was strong.

And it had led her to him.

"I still can't believe you did that," he said. "Attacked a Scorpiian with a broom."

"Well, I thought he was a dog. A freaky fairy dog. Anyway, I'm so glad I did."

"As am I. I know better than to ask you to never do something like that again. Instead, may I ask that I be allowed to train you so you can defend yourself?"

"I'd love that!"

Her enthusiasm warmed him. The moment they returned to Earth, he would begin her training.

His ship notified him that they were nearing Antares-3. He keyed in Hank's code along with the initial communication to his contact, letting them know he was on approach.

Even expecting a shipment and with Hank's code, they wouldn't be expecting *him* and there was no fooling an Antarean about what he was.

"You're nervous," Kimmy said.

Serac nodded. "Centaurans weren't well-received before the war. Now... I have no idea how they'll react to me."

She ran her fingers through his hair. His flesh pebbled as a wave of sensation swept over his entire body in response.

"It'll be fine," she said. "You have me. And I know how to talk to people."

Reassurance and confidence flowed out from her into him and just like that, all nervousness went away. He had never felt so accepted before.

He wrapped his arms around her waist tighter. "I can't believe how lucky I am that I found you."

"Actually, I found you, if you'll recall. Tussling in my backyard."

He laughed and nodded. "Either way, I'm grateful that it happened."

"Me, too."

She leaned in to kiss him again, but before she could, something soft and furry darted between them, chittering loudly.

"Payback," she said, laughing as the parcel scurried up to her shoulder again.

"He's excited to go to the planet," Serac said. "He always gets like this before runs."

Kimmy turned in Serac's lap to see out the viewports better. He could sense her excitement as well. She and the parcel were a pair in that.

"It looks like something from a sci-fi movie," she said.

The ship descended into the atmosphere. Orange clouds filled the yellow-tinted sky and tall towers of earth rose up hundreds of feet from the ground. He wove among them, heading for the rendezvous point.

Antareans flew between the towers, landing on ledges or darting into their buildings with ease—and no need for ships, with their translucent sets of wings.

"Okay, now it *really* looks like a sci-fi movie." Kimmy leaned forward to get a better look all around. "Are those gigantic termite mounds?"

An Antarean flew above the ship, close enough to see them inside the ship and wave one of her many arms at them. She hurried back on her original course.

Kimmy cringed against his chest. "What are those?"

"Those are Antareans," he said.

"Antareans are giant ant people? That's a little on-the-nose, don't you think?"

"I don't know what that means, but I don't think they have noses. Just small slits on the fronts of their faces."

"Okay…" She took a deep breath and let it out slowly. "I can do this. They seem friendly. That one even waved at us, right?"

"She did. Antareans are among the most peaceful and kind sentients in the galaxy. I think you'll like them."

"Then I'm sure I will. I just have to get past the

whole…giant ants thing. Which I absolutely can do."

Her confidence again flooded into him. He'd never met someone so sure of themselves—except maybe Hank.

A billow of red dust plumed up from beneath them. He steered around it to keep the viewport clear.

Kimmy leaned forward again, looking up at the sky this time.

"It's so… yellow," she said. "Can we breathe out there?"

"We can, but I wouldn't recommend it. We'll land in a hangar bay, where the air is purified."

A process that wouldn't be needed if it weren't for the High Council. He fought back the wave of anger at what had happened on Antares-3. Frost lined the inside of the viewport.

At least this time his cold wouldn't affect Kimmy adversely.

She rested her hand on the side of his face. "Tell me."

"I just remember the vids that my mother used to show me of Antares-3 before the Coalition came for them. The sky was bright green, and the plants were covered in vibrant yellow-orange foliage. The planet was covered with vast purple oceans that are now black and stagnant."

"That's awful."

"They resisted the influence of the High Council for a time, refusing to trade and only offering what they thought was assistance for others. But then, their ecosystems started to crumble, and they had to exchange what remained of their natural resources for the Coalition's technology just to survive."

After the assignments he'd assisted Dean with, Serac had little doubt of what had caused the ecological disaster they'd suffered so long ago.

He hadn't believed his clan's stories about how the Coalition had wronged the Centaurans and went out to see for himself. He truly wished that they had been exaggerating.

"You think the Coalition did this to them on purpose," Kimmy said.

"I do." He tightened his grip around her waist. "When I worked with Dean, he took assignments from the High Council. They were fond of using Scorpiians for their work. At first, I was only there to provide an intimidation factor."

"I don't get that. I mean, you're a big, imposing guy, but he can change into…a big imposing guy. Or anything else he wants. Why are people more afraid of you?"

"Scorpiians are limited to taking on the forms of others. They can't always replicate their abilities. And our affinity for cold can be…extreme. You've only seen the effects when I'm mildly upset. It grows stronger with the strength of the emotion."

"I'm really glad I'm immune to it now," Kimmy said.

"Our mates must be for us to protect them."

"There's more that you're not telling me," she said.

"Dean eventually wanted me to do more than intimidate," Serac said. "He started asking me to assist with his missions. When I learned their parameters…" He shook his head. "We parted ways. I never looked back."

"Until you came to Earth to see what he was up to."

"To stop him." He let out a laugh. "But then, you did that for me."

"Nobody messes with my guests," Kimmy said. "Pets are like family on Earth. People entrust them to me. I take that seriously."

"I don't doubt it."

"When we get back, we need to deal with him," Kimmy said. "I want Mrs. Simpkins's cats safe."

"They will be. We'll see to it."

He activated the sequence for their final approach to the hangar bay where they were to meet his contact. Speaking with Kimmy had put him more at ease than he'd thought possible. Her confidence spread to him.

The Antareans would accept their shipment. They would accept *him*. With Kimmy at his side, anything was possible.

Chapter Fourteen

Don't freak out. Don't freak out.

If Kimmy repeated the command enough, she'd make it happen. Or not happen. Right?

"You don't have to go," Serac said.

But she did. She could sense how much he needed her at his side. And she wanted to be there.

She just had to get over the whole…giant ants thing.

"I'll be fine." She smiled at him, willing herself to focus on the excitement of being on another planet and meeting actual aliens. Other than Serac, of course.

Her mate.

That thought lent her the strength to follow him down the ramp that led from his ship. The shipment they'd brought along was in an antigrav pallet that floated next to them.

Three Antareans waited to greet them near the ship. They really did look like giant ants. Their heads rested like sideways watermelons on their thin necks—huge, segmented eyes on either side. Their eyes glowed a pretty sky-blue. It reminded her of Payback—who was resting in the collar of her jacket again—which helped her move past the buggy-ness of them.

"Welcome to Antares-3," the tallest Antarean said. Her voice had a strange echo to it, and Kimmy could hear chittering and clicks underlying the words.

Serac had told her that instead of downloading the languages they needed straight to their brains, Antareans always wore translators. Their mouths couldn't make the sounds needed to speak most of the more common languages in the Coalition. It was freaky—and kind of cool—to hear both sets of sounds at once.

"We thank you for—" The tall Antarean's antennae stiffened suddenly and she took a step back.

The other two turned to her with obvious concern. Their eyes turned yellow as all three looked at Serac.

"For…for your shipment," the Antarean finished, in a small voice.

Serac held completely still, hands at his sides. Kimmy could sense his anguish, that longing rising up in him again. Alien or not, the need to be accepted seemed to be universal.

Kimmy stepped forward and held out a hand. "Hi," she said, as brightly as she could. "So, this is Serac, who apparently didn't think to introduce himself and I'm Kimmy. I'm from Earth. I hear you guys are really good friends with my people. I hope we can be friends as well."

"I… Thank you?" The lead Antarean shifted her attention to Kimmy, antennae twirling.

Kimmy wasn't sure if she wanted the Antarean to take her hand or not. When she reached out, Kimmy repeated, *"Don't freak out. Don't freak out,"* over and over in her head.

The Antarean's hand…claw-thing actually felt nice. It was cool and kind of velvety. She gently shook Kimmy's hand before pulling back.

"An Earthling?" the Antarean asked. "We were not expecting an Earthling."

Kimmy leaned close. "I bet you weren't expecting a Centauran, either."

All three Antareans let out a little hissing noise. They held their arms together in front of them—and they had *a lot* of arms—and bowed.

"It's understandable," Serac said. "I used my captain's code, and he is Lyrian."

"Yes," the leader said. "We were expecting Craig or Barbara."

"I follow their son, Hank."

Kimmy wanted to cover her face with her hands. Serac had all the salesmanship of a brick wall. He was standing like a soldier or a guard or something, his expression stern. No wonder Dean had used Serac for the intimidation factor—but that wasn't serving anyone now.

How could she ease the situation? They'd been expecting a Lyrian. Maybe something else from Lyra would help.

"We might not be Lyrians, but we do have this little guy." Kimmy reached up under her hair and pulled out Payback. The parcel wrapped three of his hands around her fingers, holding on tight as he gazed at the Antareans and chittered.

"A parcel!" The leader clapped several of her hands together, her eyes beaming blue again. "I've never seen one before."

"Well, this guy is as friendly as can be," Kimmy said. She cradled him closer and started tickling his belly. "He loves tickles."

Payback perked up when he heard the word. He looked around, then leaped onto the Antarean.

Kimmy panicked. What if tickles were some sort of insult here? What if Antareans didn't like them?

"Payback, no," Kimmy shouted.

He was already wriggling his fingers against the Antarean's...carapace. She cocked her head, her body arching a bit away from the parcel. She made a little tittering sound.

"I'm so sorry," Kimmy said, trying to grab Payback.

"It is...not unpleasant." The Antarean plucked Payback from her side with one of many, many arms. She began petting him, and he cooed and leaned against her. "I would not say it was pleasant, either, however."

"Serac told me parcels are really good at finding nerve clusters," Kimmy said.

"I didn't know that parcels ever left their Lyrian families," the Antarean said, her eyes turning a deep magenta that matched Payback's fur.

Kimmy leaned forward and mock-whispered, "I think I've been adopted."

The Antarean's antennae kept shifting between pointing at Payback and then back to Serac. Kimmy wasn't sure she'd quite won them over yet.

"But I guess we should get back to business," Kimmy said.

The Antarean handed Payback over, then turned to Serac, clasping her hands in front of her. Her antennae now pointed straight at him, though she kept her head somewhat bowed.

In a booming voice, Serac said, "We offer this shipment as a show of good faith." He gestured at the antigrav pallet.

Oh boy.

She was really going to have to work with him on his business presentations.

"Craig and Barbara are occupied assisting the Department of Homeworld Security on Earth," he went on. "We would like to take over their trade routes to bring you the supplies you need."

The leader looked to the other two Antareans. Their eyes strobed and their antennae twirled and twitched. Kimmy was sure they were having a conversation—and a heated one at that.

"Your offer is most kind," the leader said.

Kimmy sensed a *but*, and not a good *but*. She didn't give them a chance to turn Serac away.

"Isn't it?" she said, stepping between the Antareans and Serac. "Serac has been explaining everything to me, and I'm just overwhelmed at how much you all look after each other. The cooperation between..." Dangit, what was the word?

"Sentients," Serac helpfully offered.

"Sentients," Kimmy said. "Right. Your cooperation is inspiring. It gives me hope for our future, knowing that Earth is working with such selfless and generous people."

She stepped back to stand by Serac, looping her arm around his and hugging it while leaning close into his side. She cast the biggest, brightest smile she could at the Antareans.

"You..." the leader began. "Your pheromones... You are mated."

Kimmy could feel her cheeks heat. Her smile probably dimmed a bit, but she knew it was more sincere.

She looked up at Serac, and said, "Yes, we are."

"The bond is new," the Antarean said.

"Umm... yes." Kimmy's face must have been bright red. What else could the Antareans sense?

"This is to be celebrated!" the leader said. "A union between an Earthling and a Centauran is surely a sign of peace."

"I hope so," Kimmy said. "But we have a long path ahead. And speaking of that, as much as we'd both love to stay here and celebrate, we should be heading back to Earth."

She let go of Serac's arm and then gently steered the antigrav pallet closer to the Antareans, figuring they probably didn't want him getting closer. As soon as it was in reach, the lead Antarean opened it. Her eyes turned bright blue as she saw the shipment they had brought.

Kimmy had never thought that anyone could be so excited over dirt and seeds, but all three Antareans gathered around, their hands clasped solemnly in front of their torsos.

"Our scientists will begin replicating the microbiomes present in these samples immediately," the leader said. "Between that and the seeds, we should be able to increase our planetary food production to the point of self-sufficiency once more. You have done our people a great service."

Where did they get their food if they couldn't grow enough of their own? Was the Coalition helping them?

With everything Kimmy had learned about the High Council, even with it being gone, she was nervous about the Antareans being reliant on the Coalition for food. What if another awful faction took over? What if something happened that stopped the Coalition from bringing them the food they needed?

The two Antareans who hadn't spoken reached in and carefully picked up what was within the antigrav pallet. They bowed low to Kimmy. Not knowing what else to do, she bowed back.

"Your payment." The lead Antarean held out a hand. She was holding something that looked like a glowing ball of amber.

Whatever it was, a spike of wonder and amazement jumped from Serac to Kimmy, threaded with a tinge of regret.

"I can't accept that," Serac said. "This shipment is a gift."

"But, the seeds," the Antarean said. "Their worth—"

"As much as I think I'm going to regret turning that down when I find out what it is," Kimmy said, "what we seek in return is friendship and a chance to help more."

Kimmy couldn't believe it, but she was all-in. Now that she knew what was at stake, she totally understood why Serac and his crew couldn't wait to assist people— sentients—like the Antareans. It was worth the risks.

She wanted to do even more to help them return their ecosystems to health. And *now*.

"Serac mentioned that you're having a problem with your oceans," Kimmy said.

The leader's eyes strobed a deep indigo. "Yes, we are."

"Well, is there something we can do?" Kimmy asked.

"Different dirt or something?"

"You are a most generous sentient," the Antarean said. "We have cleared our oceans of the toxins we discovered within them, but have not made further progress. The Department of Homeworld Security is sending an assessment team to see how they can assist us, but they have other priorities as well. Between that and the war… It may be some time before work begins restoring our waters."

Nope, nope, nope.

"Tell me what you need," Kimmy said. "I can't make any promises beyond I'll do whatever I can."

The leader seemed hesitant to speak, but then said, "We have…sources on Earth who tell us of a plant called kelp. And there are microorganisms known as plankton. Our scientists are prepared to adapt their physiology to our homeworld, and believe this will be the foundation for restoring our oceans."

Kimmy didn't even know how she could get plankton and seaweed, especially living in Kansas, but dammit, if it helped restore an entire planet's oceans, she'd find a way.

She suddenly remembered the gold Serac had offered to Marvin, a huge smile stretching across her face. She held out her hand again, not hesitating at all to grasp the leader's claw-thing this time.

"I'll do whatever I can," Kimmy said.

Chapter Fifteen

The entire trip back to Earth had been filled with Kimmy's *chatter* as she called it. Serac delighted in listening to the outpouring of her mind and heart, especially when he had changed into his standard outfit—which Kimmy thought was "very Han Solo," whatever that meant.

For how much she seemed to like it, she'd removed it quickly to spend hours in each other's arms.

Serac had no complaints.

Now they were dressed again. He was glad to have a blaster at his side.

Kimmy had so many questions, and even more ideas. By the time they landed in her backyard, they had a plan in place to use the gold ore meant as Marvin's payment to secure streams that would preserve Earth's resources while helping to restore at least a dozen other planets. She even wanted to help Centaurus-10.

Brave, beautiful, intelligent, and so generous.

He was incredibly lucky being mated to her.

She led him into her kitchen, where all of this had begun so very recently.

"We should use some of the money from selling that ore to build a garage for your ship," Kimmy said as he shut the door.

She set the box of cereal she'd brought along on the table. Payback jumped off her shoulder, then knocked the box over and crawled inside. Kimmy just shook her head.

"I guess it would be more of a barn, with how big that is," she said. "I've always wanted a barn! But with animals in it. Maybe we can manage both? Your ship and animals?"

"Whatever you desire," Serac said.

She turned to him and smiled. "I like the sound of that. Will you be okay with this being our den, though?"

His chest tightened. "That would be wonderful. Your home is very comfortable."

She set her bag on the floor, then took the stack of blankets he carried and dropped them on top of it. With the space cleared between them, she took the opportunity to step in close, wrap her arms around his neck and rise on her toes to kiss him.

Just before their lips met, she said, "*Our* home."

Her words seared through him, lighting up every cell in his body. This was *their* home. But, truly, *she* was his home—wherever she was in the universe.

Her lips parted as he thrust his tongue into her mouth, savoring her warmth. He lifted her from the floor and she wrapped her legs around his waist.

The bedroom was just upstairs. He headed that way, but froze when Payback growled from deep in the cereal box.

Serac broke off the kiss and he and Kimmy looked over at the table. Payback burst out of the box, scattering cereal everywhere. He scrambled to the edge of the table, then back again, looking around frantically.

"What's gotten into you?" Kimmy slid down Serac's chest, then made her way to the table. She picked up the parcel, who was still growling. He was looking at the archway leading to the living room.

Serac drew his blaster. "Stay here."

"Like hell." Kimmy held Payback close and ran to grab her broom.

Dean knew that Serac was protecting Kimmy. The Scorpiian should know not to mess with her. But then, he didn't know they were mated.

Serac cautiously stepped into the living room. Dean was standing near a large set of windows that overlooked the front yard. One hand was in his pocket.

"Good morning," Dean said.

"What do you want?" Serac lifted his blaster.

"Is that how you greet me now?" Dean said. "We used to be friends."

Serac had thought so, too.

"Show me your hands," Serac said.

Dean snorted and shook his head. He lifted both hands and held them where Serac could see.

"So little trust," Dean said. "What happened to shifters having to stick together?"

"That doesn't mean we hurt other sentients." Serac stepped farther into the room. He could sense Kimmy hovering in the archway to the kitchen, intent on protecting him.

"Our mate is fierce," his *zyln* thought.

"We never did hurt others," Dean said. "We just gave them the opportunity to hurt themselves through greed and ignorance."

Serac shook his head. "It was fear and manipulation. The High Council excelled at that."

"It doesn't matter what you call it," Dean said. "They made the choices. Not us."

"There isn't an us," Serac said. "There hasn't been for a long time."

"But there could be again." Dean smiled and stepped forward, his gait relaxed. "Don't you miss it? Going wherever we wanted. Answering only to ourselves."

Serac shook his head. "Until I had to answer to my conscience."

"You think I don't have a conscience?" Dean said. "I do. I always have. It was my priorities that were different."

"Obtaining resources," Serac said.

"Protecting our team." Dean shook his head. "You were my priority. Our operation was my priority." He stepped closer, aggressive now, pointing at Serac as he went on.

"You're not the only one who was cast aside by your people. The difference between us is that *you* cast *me* aside. I thought we were brothers."

"I..." Serac didn't know what to say.

Dean had always been aloof with him, but then, Scorpiians weren't known for sharing their emotions. The thought that Serac had betrayed a bond he didn't even know existed caused a sharp pain to cross through his chest.

"I'm sorry," Serac said. "But if I had told you my concerns, would you have changed anything?"

Dean shook his head. "I guess we'll never know."

He held Serac's gaze for a few moments, then slapped the center of his chest. Serac heard a metallic click. He tried to leap back, but it was too late.

The floor came rushing up with bruising speed. His body was crushed against it, gravity pressing down on him everywhere. He cried out as the force increased, making his joints pop and his innards feel like they were in a vise.

A high shriek drowned out his cries as Kimmy ran toward him. He could hear her footsteps, but couldn't turn to see her. He couldn't warn her away.

She skidded to a stop, then something clacked on the floor and she let out a yelp. Had her broom hit the field first?

He heard her struggle for a few moments, then she crawled to where he could see her. Her eyes were filled with tears.

He had to free himself. But how could he escape the gravity well? It was too powerful even for his *zyln* to work against.

"What are you doing?" Kimmy screamed. "You're killing him."

"Centaurans are tougher than that," Dean said. "But a few amplifications and he'll be a pool of jelly on your floor."

Dean sat in one of the overstuffed chairs in the living room, pulling out the device he was using—a large, bronze disc. "You ever talk with a Sadirian? What they make up for in arrogance they lack in imagination. Antigrav pallets are great, but if you take one of these things and flip it, you can make a localized gravity field ten, twenty, a hundred times stronger than whatever normal gravity a planet has."

"Turn it off," she begged. "Please turn it off."

"Grown attached to him, have you? Good. I'll make you a deal. I'll let him go when you get me the cats."

Kimmy blinked the tears from her eyes and stared at Dean for a few moments.

"Oh my God," she yelled. "What is it with those cats?"

"I believe you Earthlings have an expression…" Dean said. "'Time's wasting.'"

"Okay, okay," Kimmy said. "You win. I'll get you the

cats, but just ease up on him."

"I don't think so. I let up a bit and he'll be able to freeze me after you leave. The pain will keep him controlled. You better hurry, though. I'm not sure just how much of this he can stand."

Kimmy stood and started toward the door. She had to thread her way between the coffee table and couch. She slowed as she neared Dean. What was she planning?

Serac could feel her growing fear and excitement. Her determination to save him. He wanted her to just leave and be safe.

"One more thing, though." She paused and reached up to rub the back of her neck. With surprising speed, she tossed something toward Dean—a bright red something—and said, "Payback, tickles!"

Dean leaped up from the chair, but not before the parcel landed on him. Payback scurried up Dean's chest and disappeared down the back of his shirt. Dean reached for the disk, but before he could modify it, his eyes widened and he doubled over.

Serac knew that Dean's clothing was actually part of his body. What Serac didn't know was how they were connected. He couldn't imagine what Dean must have been feeling at that moment.

As Dean spun in circles, his arms distending wildly as he tried to reach the parcel, Serac could see a little lump scurrying around under Dean's jacket and shirt.

"Make it stop!" Dean yelled, between bouts of... laughing.

Serac had never heard Dean laugh. The Scorpiian could barely breathe.

Dean dropped the gravity disk, and Kimmy darted forward to pick it up. Dean tried to grab her, but then let out a particularly loud laugh and fell to the floor.

"Please, make it stop," Dean said, gasping.

"First, tell me how to release Serac."

"Turn it sunwise," he said.

"Sunwise? You mean clockwise?"

Dean's face suddenly contorted, his body shrinking into the form of an older man with a bushy gray mustache and thick glasses. As he continued to laugh, he morphed again, but this time into a thin, green-tinged humanoid.

Kimmy ran toward Serac and dropped to her knees next to him. "Is this direction right?" She gestured above the disk in a direction that would crush Serac.

She gasped as she must have felt his spike of fear.

"Okay," she said. "Not that direction."

She placed her finger on the disk and ran it in a circle over its surface. The gravity pinning him to the floor lessened.

The moment he was free of it, he grabbed the disk from her and snapped it in half.

"Whoa," she said. Then her hands were on his face, her lips on his. "Are you okay? That was so scary. Tell me you're okay."

It was hard to, with her kissing him, but he managed a muffled, "I'm okay."

They heard a thud, and then a low growl. Payback came scurrying over to them—his fur bright yellow. He climbed up Kimmy's arm, running behind her hair and squeaking softly.

Serac turned toward the growl to see Dean in his quryl form. His head was low, tentacles lashing at the curtains behind him, his lips peeled back from his teeth.

Serac stood slowly, bringing Kimmy up to stand next to him. He noticed that her fingers had curled around the handle of her broom. She was ready to fight, his fierce mate.

"It doesn't have to be this way," Serac said. "Leave now. Never threaten us again."

Dean growled, then leaped at them.

Kimmy shrieked, "Look out," trying to push Serac away.

He held her tight against his side, lifting his free arm toward Dean and letting all of his rage and grief at the loss of their friendship blast out of him—as well as his desire to protect Kimmy above all else.

Dean froze mid-jump, ice coating his body and locking him to the floor. The entire room was covered in a thin layer of frost—windows, furniture, floor.

For a moment, neither of them said a word. Then

Kimmy stepped a bit away from him, turning in a slow circle.

"Oh, wow," she said. "It's like an ice castle." She ran her finger over the couch. "Everything is going to get so wet when it thaws."

"We can fix it."

She smiled at him. "I know."

She turned back to Dean and looked at him more closely. When the Scorpiian blinked his many eyes, she leaped back and yelped.

"He's still alive?" she asked.

"Scorpiians are hard to kill." Serac pulled her against his side again. He glared at Dean, pushing as much menace as he could into his expression. "Kimmy and I have bonded."

He paused for a few moments to let that sink in. Dean closed his eyes for a few moments, then opened them.

"I don't have to hold back to keep her safe," Serac said. "And next time, I won't."

"This is you *holding back*?" she asked.

Serac squeezed her tighter against his side, keeping his attention on Dean.

"For the friendship we once had, I will let you go," Serac said. "But I don't want to see you again."

Kimmy leaned forward. "And you have to promise to leave Mrs. Simpkins's cats alone."

Serac could sense that she was trying to exude

menace...not quite successfully. He drew from his own experience and broadcast as much threat as he could, using all the intimidation skills he'd learned over the years.

"Blink if you understand," Serac said.

Dean hesitated for a long while, but finally blinked.

Serac nodded, then took the broom from Kimmy and struck the ice holding the Scorpiian in place, breaking it to pieces.

The moment Dean's claws hit the ground, he turned and leaped through the bay windows. Glass shattered into the front yard.

"Hey," Kimmy yelled. "You couldn't use the door?"

"We'll fix it," Serac said, pulling her close again.

"Fine. But he should pay for it."

"That would mean we would see him again. And I doubt we will."

Kimmy shook her head. "I guess time will tell."

Chapter Sixteen

"So, let me be sure I understand." Hank's booming voice made Kimmy want to cringe. It was only Serac's tight grip on her hand that helped her stay steady. The Lyrian was imposing, even when viewed through a vid screen.

"I sent you to investigate the communication from this Dean fellow, to scout out trade routes, and to deliver my family's parcel to my new sibling," Hank said. "Instead—without my authorization—you moved forward with establishing a relationship with a respected supplier on Earth and made our first delivery to the Antareans, securing our role as their new trade partners."

"Yes," Serac said.

"And the Scorpiian?" Hank asked.

"No longer a threat," Serac said. "To our operations, at least."

"Hmm." Even that sound from the Lyrian boomed through Serac's ship, the noise making Kimmy's chest vibrate.

"And in the"—Hank made a point of looking at a control panel on his chair—"seventy-two Earth hours that you've been gone from my ship, you also became mated to an Earthling."

"Yes." Serac squeezed her hand, sending waves of calm and confidence through her. It was wonderful to feel from him.

"Given everything Serac has accomplished, I think you should assign him as part of a permanent presence on Earth," Kimmy said.

Serac opened his mouth to speak, but then just let out a breath and smiled at her.

Hank's eyebrow ridge rose up his forehead. "She certainly is a bold sentient."

"She's not afraid to speak up for herself—or others." Serac turned to address her. "You'll make an excellent partner for our operations. If you're comfortable with them, that is."

"I am." She leaned in closer, mesmerized by the way the light was gleaming across his lips.

Hank cleared his throat loudly. "What is it with Earth and these pair-bonds?"

Payback poked his head out from Kimmy's hair and chittered at them in a chiding tone.

"Anything else you'd like to tell me?" Hank asked.

"About the parcel—" Serac halted as Kimmy cut him off.

"I accidentally imprinted with him," Kimmy said.

"Accidentally?" Hank repeated.

"And then trained him to attack using something the Earthlings call tickles," Serac said. "He will be an even more useful companion for your sibling—when she's of age to have a parcel."

Hank huffed out a breath, then rubbed his chin with one of his hands. "There must be more to this Earthling than it seems. Very well. You are assigned to Earth for the foreseeable future. You and your mate can work together to secure that end of our supply chain."

Kimmy's heart felt like it was in her throat. They could be together and still help others and she could run her pet parlor and... and...everything.

"I expect regular reports, incredible success, and you"—he fixed Kimmy with a pointed stare—"will take *excellent* care of my family's parcel. Understood?"

She stood a little straighter. "Yes, sir."

Hank let out a snort and turned back to Serac. "The Department of Homeworld Security is looking to set up a permanent presence in Harbor. It will be harder for you to operate outside their scans, but we can't have them slowing us down. They can help others as they are able, but need to leave us to do our own good."

She could sense Serac preparing a response, but Kimmy jumped in again. She wanted them to know that she was Serac's partner in this. His equal.

"Absolutely," Kimmy said. "We understand the importance of...expediting the recovery of whatever planets we can."

Hank leaned back in his chair and grinned. "I like her. In that case, welcome to the crew, Kimmy."

He ended the transmission.

"I'm part of the crew?" Kimmy asked.

"According to our captain."

"Part of a spaceship crew?"

"Last I checked."

"And you get to stay with me!" Her excitement echoed back at her from Serac.

"I do," he said.

"This is really happening."

"It is."

He rested his hands on her waist, leaning in so their foreheads touched. A low growl of approval rumbled from his chest.

"Well, in that case..." She wrapped her arms around his neck, pulling him closer. Just before their lips met, she said, "Welcome home."

—

Thank you so much for reading *Rate of Return*! There are so many exciting adventures ahead, starting off with a foray into a brand new spin-off series! The *Cygnian 7* series launches in 2021. They're big, they're blue, and when it comes to the soulmates they're finding on Earth, they're completely clueless. I hope you'll join us as they figure things out! Enjoy this sneak peek into the first book of the series, *Nuar: A Scifi Alien Warriors Romance*.

Nuar: A Scifi Alien Warriors Romance

Cygnian 7
Book One

Chapter One

Earth was a confusing mess. Nuar couldn't figure out why Kral had dragged all of the warriors in their prism to this backwards planet in the middle of nowhere.

Actually, it was worse than the middle of nowhere. It was well inside Coalition territory. The planet was crawling with Sadirians. The Earthlings themselves were almost identical to the oppressive aliens they had welcomed into their system.

As far as Nuar could tell, none of the Earthlings realized their mistake. They were carrying on their lives as they had since their industrial revolution, almost all of the population not even aware that aliens walked among them, let alone that their planet was one of the few that remained untouched by the galactic war.

Kral should be warning them that they were in a different kind of danger. The Coalition would strip this planet bare of resources and absorb the populace into their own. And that was if Earth was lucky.

With the Tau Centauran Assembly fighting against the Coalition, and winning, by all accounts, the Earthlings could meet with an even darker fate. Nuar felt a twinge of pity for them at the thought of the Tau Ceti colonizing the planet, setting up their wretched spawning pools, and absorbing the populace in their own way—as a food source.

Cygnus-Prime shouldn't be getting anywhere near this mess. So why were Kral and his prism—Nuar included in that honored group—following a Sadirian female on a "tour" of this low-tech, socially stunted planet?

They were heading down a wide walkway that led from the hangar where their ship was located toward a small town called Harbor. The Sadirian's short blonde hair bounced along her shoulders as she walked. She cast a bright smile at them that Nuar absolutely did not trust.

Earth had informally sided with the Coalition of Planets. It remained to be seen whether humans were as corrupt as Sadirians or just too foolish to realize the danger they represented.

Nuar's experience with humans was limited to members of the Department of Homeworld Security. He still hadn't made up his mind about Earthlings, but kept his eyes open as he followed along on the tour.

Perhaps it was a trap instead. That would be interesting.

As much as he believed his people should stay out of Earth's business, he relished the idea of being able to test his strength and skills against a new opponent. The Earthlings were no threat and their weapons useless against a Cygnian, but they were rumored to have attracted a variety of other species to their planet.

His spirits somewhat lifted, Nuar looked around with renewed interest, seeking challenges or enemies. All he saw was grass, dirt, trees, and a cluster of buildings ahead.

A gentle breeze swept over him, countering the summer temperature—not that it was a problem for Nuar or any of the other Cygnians. Earth's small yellow star cast pitifully low amounts of radiation through the atmosphere. It was no wonder all the life forms on the planet were so weak.

Earth was excessively comfortable.

The sky was unsettling, though. The same blue as Nuar, Dorn, and Rom's skin. The other four members of the prism were a darker blue, with Lar a rich cobalt, like their queen.

"We're so happy that you chose to come," the Sadirian

was saying. What was her name again? Right. Vay.

Nuar hoped he wouldn't have to remember it for long. There couldn't be much to see in such a small town. Earth had nothing to offer them.

"We've been getting everything ready for months," Vay continued the steady stream of her conversation. "It's an honor to have your entire prism visiting Earth. Is it true that Cygnians have seven possible eye colors?"

"It is," Lar said.

Nuar felt his chest swell with pride as he thought of the full spectrum represented in his group—a rare complete prism—from Rom's violet eyes to Nuar's own spectral red. The Cygnian population had been dwindling for several generations. Finding fellow warriors whose unique soul-frequencies could harmonize with each others' was becoming more rare.

Finding a soulmate was out of the question.

Vay glanced at the warriors with her, her brow furrowing. Nuar glared when their eyes met, and she quickly looked away.

"Tarn is with the ship," Lar said. "He prefers his engineering bay to new planets."

"I see." Vay's smile was a bit strained. Nuar felt a surge of sympathy for her. He quickly crushed it.

"I was surprised not to see him with the group, since Kral is your crown prince," Vay said.

Bron let out a low growl. The vibration spread out from

him, resonating in the plates that covered Nuar's spine. Nuar forced them to stay folded against his back rather than risk tearing through the thin fabric of the Earth clothing Kral had asked them to wear.

"We travel with him because he's our friend, not because he's our prince," Bron said. "He doesn't need bodyguards."

"I didn't mean any offense." Vay's pale blue eyes grew round. "I guess I don't understand the prism bond that well, but I'd love to learn more. I am the cultural liaison, after all. Not that I wouldn't be interested otherwise. I mean, having such a close connection among your group of warriors sounds wonderful."

She barely stopped to breathe as she spoke. Irritating. Primarily because the more she spoke, the harder it was for Nuar to not like her.

He wanted to get this over with. He needed to be... somewhere. Back at his ship, perhaps. Except, he wanted to keep going forward. Deeper into the town.

A strange feeling was nagging at the back of his mind and making him uneasy. It was probably just from knowing there were so many Sadirians and their allies lurking around. Still, it was unsettling.

"I hope you'll accept my apology." Vay clasped her hands in front of her chest as she stopped next to the first building at the edge of town.

Bron had been paying more attention to the

environment than the Sadirian leading their group and had to stop abruptly to keep from running into her. Nuar, however, plowed into Bron's back, knocking his fellow warrior forward a few paces.

Bron had to flail his arms and stagger to the side to keep from crushing Vay. It was one of the funniest things Nuar had seen in a while. The group laughed, some of their tense energy unraveling.

"Your turn, then." Bron shoved Nuar, hard.

They both laughed as Nuar nearly lost his footing, flailing in much the same way to avoid the Sadirian in their midst. Dorn stepped in front of her, their security officer always focused on keeping others safe.

It was good to have a distraction. The familiar physical challenge was a much nicer focus than their strange surroundings or that nagging feeling of *need* in the back of Nuar's mind.

"Are you up for an experiment, science officer?" Nuar said with a grin.

Bron arched an eyebrow and asked, "What did you have in mind?"

"Let's see how far I can throw you on this low gravity world," Nuar said.

Bron bared his teeth in a broad smile, setting his feet apart and waiting for Nuar's charge. Rom stepped between them, his hands raised to keep them apart.

"Stop playing around," Rom said.

Nuar straightened. "We're not playing. This is an *experiment*."

"No, this is you being bored and trying to find something to do," Rom said. "As usual."

"I'm the medic for a group of near-invulnerable warriors," Nuar said. "I'm always bored."

Rom stepped right up in Nuar's space, nose-to-nose as he issued his challenge. "Find a more constructive outlet."

The Sadirian chose that moment to join the conversation. "I think I'm going about this wrong," she said.

She dropped her hands to her sides, glancing back and forth between Rom and Nuar. She pressed her lips together in a determined line, then yelled, "Like I'd think Kral needed a guard!"

She reached out and braced her hands on the closest Cygnian's chest, which happened to be Lar's, and shoved him.

Rather, she tried to. Lar didn't budge.

Nuar had to hand it to the Sadirian, though. She pushed hard enough that she knocked herself backward, landing right against Kral's chest.

Kral caught her to help her keep her balance. He arched an eyebrow at the prism, his orange eyes gleaming with mirth. For a moment, he grinned at them above her head where she couldn't see, then forced his expression to look dour and disapproving again.

"Bron accepts your apology," Kral said, keeping his voice low.

Bron grunted.

Kral bared his teeth, his disapproval most likely becoming real. "Bron accepts your apology." He bit out each word.

With another low growl, Bron inclined his head slightly. "Of course."

"I… Thank you." Vay pulled her lower lip between her teeth for a moment, then let out a sigh. "I just want you to feel comfortable here."

"Comfort is not an issue." Nuar snorted. "This entire planet is coated in soft things."

He reached over to the building next to them and snapped off a corner of one of the blocks it appeared to be made of. Grinding his fingers against his palm, he watched as the material turned to a russet powder.

"Let's maybe not crush the buildings' bricks," Vay said. "Most of these structures aren't made of advanced durable materials."

"We can see that," Bron said.

"Harbor is an example of what's possible if we all work together," Vay said. "We did our best to preserve the existing Earth structures, improving them with designs proposed by humans and using Vegan technology."

Nuar stifled a snort. He still didn't believe there were actual Vegans on the planet, despite the rumors. He glanced over at Bron, who was also stifling a smirk.

Vay went on, oblivious. "And the Antareans were amazingly helpful in the construction."

The plates running along Nuar's spine started to rise. Judging by how the other warriors' stances changed, most were dealing with the same reaction.

"You used the Antareans?" Lar's tone was thick with disapproval.

"We didn't *use* anyone," Vay said, an intriguing challenge to her voice. "The Antareans *offered* and the Earthlings of this town gratefully accepted their help in exchange for supplies and resources that have helped the Antarean homeworld immensely."

Vay gestured down the road to a tall building made of similar red blocks—bricks—but wrapped with large brown tunnels built onto the walls in winding spirals. Small plants grew from the tops and sides of the tunnels, and more greenery could be seen on top of the roof.

"You're welcome to talk to them yourself," she said. "Several have decided to settle here and make Harbor their home. They live in that apartment building along with humans, Sadirians, and Vegans."

Nuar saw movement on the roof of the building. Two of the insectoid Antareans walked to the edge of the building, their antennae pointing toward Nuar's group. One was holding a large pot with a plant in it. They both lifted some of their many arms and waved.

"Greetings, Vay," one of them shouted.

"Hello Sisters," Vay yelled, waving back. "Your rooftop garden is looking great!"

"Thank you," the other Antarean replied. Their giant, segmented eyes strobed a happy pink. "We look forward to planting Lian's latest seedlings once they are ready." They waved again before heading back toward the center of the roof and out of sight.

Vay turned to the prism and said, "Please don't mistake the Coalition for the High Council. The High Council is gone and…" she lifted her chin, "good riddance to them."

With every word, Nuar liked her more, no matter how much he didn't want to. His desire to leave the planet also grew. They should not be getting involved in any of this.

"The *Coalition* does not take advantage of sentients," Vay said. "We take care of each other. We work—and live —together. That's Harbor. And if you don't like it…" She seemed to struggle to find the right word. When she did, she stiffened her spine and crossed her arms over her chest. "Tough cookies."

Lar looked at Kral and mouthed, "Tough cookies?"

Kral laughed. Nuar felt his spine plates relax. He still didn't trust the Coalition, but this Sadirian… This Sadirian, he liked.

The High Council might be gone, but their influence most likely remained among their people. They couldn't have changed that much in such a short amount of time.

"The town is a fine accomplishment," Kral said. "It's good to see these sentients working together."

"We're very proud of what we've done here," Vay said.

"As you should be." Kral laughed again, then pulled Vay against his side with an arm draped over her shoulders. Her eyes widened, but she didn't protest.

"One thing, though," Kral said. "What are cookies?"

Vay beamed at him, her eyes crinkling at the corners. "Cygnus X, they are the best thing in the universe." She clamped a hand over her mouth for a moment, then said, "Pardon my language."

Kral just smiled.

"Are they a weapon?" Bron asked.

She pinched her lips between her teeth, then burst out with a laugh. "No, they're a food. A delicious food. We can pick some up at the bakery. It's just down the street."

They started along the paved path again, passing buildings with clear viewports that made up most of their front walls. Nuar glanced around as Vay described the operations within them, not really listening.

His gaze lit on a large, white, multi-armed form across the street. Was that a Lyrian?

"I'll catch up in a moment," Nuar said.

Bron shrugged, then followed Vay and the other warriors into one of the buildings.

Excitement teased the edges of Nuar's nerves. His

hearts pounded a dual beat in either side of his chest.

Finally, something of interest.

Lyrians rarely left their planet. Nuar had never seen one, though he'd studied everything he could about them.

Lyrians could camouflage themselves so well, they would be undetectable through any physical or technological means. Not even Cygnian holographic technology could rival a Lyrian's natural defense.

Their strength and resilience was legendary. This one was seven feet tall—as tall as Nuar—but three times as thick in the chest.

Few Cygnians had ever had a chance to try their might against a Lyrian.

Nuar crossed the street quickly, coming up behind the Lyrian as he turned around a corner. Nuar hurried to catch up with him.

The moment Nuar rounded the corner, four strong hands gripped him and lifted him off his feet. He found himself staring into eyes as dark blue as Tarn's, set in a pale blue face surrounded by bristling white fur.

The Lyrian pulled his lips back from his many small, serrated teeth in a smile. "Hello, Cygnian," he said. "Would you care to explain why you're trying to sneak up on me?

Nuar laughed. "Cygnians don't sneak. I was approaching you to introduce myself. I am Nuar."

The Lyrian pursed his lips and snorted out a breath

through the nostrils in his flat face. His winglike ears twitched as he set Nuar down and released him.

"I'm Craig," the Lyrian said.

"Well met, Craig." Nuar extended his hand.

Craig's brow ridge arched on one side. He gripped Nuar's hand in the Earth-style greeting Nuar had been trained to use, but then clasped Nuar's elbow with one of his other hands.

"Are you supposed to be here, Nuar?" Craig asked. "Vay's been talking for weeks about the tour she has planned for you all."

Nuar waved his free hand dismissively. "My prism can sense where I am. And I doubt the Sadirian will even notice my departure."

"Hmm." Craig tightened his grips. "Interesting that you call her 'the Sadirian,' when you know she has a name."

"I also know she's with the Coalition." Nuar tightened his grip as well. Tighter than the grip he'd used to pulverize the brick. The Lyrian was unfazed.

Craig smirked. "Did you also know that Vay is my daughter?"

Nuar felt his jaw drop. The Coalition was infamous for their genetic experiments, but creating a Sadirian linked with Lyrian DNA? How had the Coalition even obtained it?

Nuar had thought that the Lyrians were one of the few sentient species fortunate enough to have eluded the High

Council's lust for more genetic material to experiment upon. Then again, until recently, Nuar had thought the Cygnians had managed to escape that fate as well. He was wrong.

His spines began to rise again at the thought of what the High Council had done to one of their own. Craig's grip tightened further, perhaps noticing Nuar's distress.

Nuar stammered a few half-formed words, his mind refusing to provide anything helpful besides, "How?"

"This planet has a very strange effect on unmated sentients," Craig said. His voice became a bit wistful as he went on. "My mate and I adopted an orphaned human we found wandering the woods alone and unprotected. When he met Vay, they pair-bonded. They are now married, both according to Sadirian and Earth customs."

"I see," Nuar said. That made a lot more sense than the scenarios he'd been considering.

Craig pulled Nuar closer, so that their faces were inches apart. "I'm not sure you do. Vay has been very excited about today. She's worked tirelessly to prepare for your arrival, barely having time to spend with our family and our new nestling. And yet, you're here, and she's there. Which I'm concerned might disappoint her."

Nuar smiled, his hearts pounding at the thought of a true challenge. "If you'd like, you're welcome to try to get me from here to there."

Craig's lips pulled into a toothy smile again. "I would

love to."

—

Nuar and the rest of the Cygnian Warriors begin arriving in the Fall of 2021. Be sure you catch up on all of *The Department of Homeworld Security* adventures before then! You can get many of the novellas in the first two series omnibuses, *The Department of Homeworld Security Omnibus 1* and *The Department of Homeworld Security Omnibus 2.*

I'd love to keep in touch. Join my newsletter at sendfox.com/cassandrachandler to hear about all the adventures happening in Cassland. And if you enjoyed this book, please consider leaving a review at your favorite book review site. I'd really appreciate it—reviews help readers and authors alike!

Thank you for reading *Rate of Return!*

Cassandra Chandler

About the Author

USA Today Bestselling author Cassandra Chandler uses her vivid imagination to make the world more interesting, spawning the ideas she turns into her whimsical Science Fiction Romances and darkly evocative Paranormal and Urban Fantasy Romances. Fast-paced and funny, lighthearted or dark, her stories will introduce you to characters you'll fall in love with and worlds you long to explore.

www.ingramcontent.com/pod-product-compliance
Lightning Source LLC
Chambersburg PA
CBHW051242170626
46809CB00004B/1450